"Trust me, Tessa."

As if he'd sensed her continued trepidation, he stopped again before they reached the SUV. "We're going to rescue the children. That's why I came."

Mixed emotions twisted in her chest. All this time she'd been certain no one was coming. That there wasn't anyone out there big enough or brave enough to be the savior she'd prayed for.

Yet here was this man, standing right in front of her, claiming to be exactly what she'd asked for.

She couldn't help herself. She hugged him. "Thank you."

His arms went around her, held her tight. "Those aren't the only reasons I came."

She drew back, looked into his eyes. "I don't understand."

"I came for you."

DEBRA WEBB

COLBY CORE

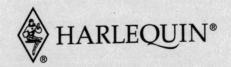

HARLEQUIN®

TORONTO • NEW YORK • LONDON
AMSTERDAM • PARIS • SYDNEY • HAMBURG
STOCKHOLM • ATHENS • TOKYO • MILAN • MADRID
PRAGUE • WARSAW • BUDAPEST • AUCKLAND

This story is dedicated to the families of all the missing children around the world. God be with you. No one should suffer this heinous tragedy.

Recycling programs
for this product may
not exist in your area.

ISBN-13: 978-0-373-74568-5

COLBY CORE

Copyright © 2010 by Debra Webb

ABOUT THE AUTHOR

Debra Webb wrote her first story at age nine and her first romance at thirteen. It wasn't until she spent three years working for the military behind the Iron Curtain and within the confining political walls of Berlin, Germany, that she realized her true calling. A five-year stint with NASA on the Space Shuttle Program reinforced her love of the endless possibilities within her grasp as a storyteller. A collision course between suspense and romance was set. Debra has been writing romantic suspense and action-packed romantic thrillers since. Visit her at www.DebraWebb.com or write to her at P.O. Box 4889, Huntsville, AL 35815.

Books by Debra Webb

CAST OF CHARACTERS

Riley Porter—Former military, Riley isn't afraid of dying to get the job done.

Tessa Woods—Her life was stolen. She had hoped and prayed for a hero. Can Riley fill those shoes?

The Master—A ruthless man who grows rich marketing children.

Brooks and Howard—Ambitious and merciless deputies who obey the Master's every order.

Levi Stark—The Colby Agency investigator assigned to provide backup to Porter.

Moses—The man claims to be a doctor...but can he be trusted?

Renwick—The Master's archenemy. He will do anything to kill the competition.

Phipps—Renwick's right-hand man. He wants more from Tessa than information.

Sophie—An innocent child trapped between good and evil.

Agent Ross—An FBI agent determined to bring down the Master, but will he be more reliable than his predecessor in the first phase of this operation?

Jim Colby and Victoria Colby-Camp—Mother and son, as a team they run the most elite private investigations agency in the business.

Chapter One

Saturday, December 26, 10:00 p.m.

New Orleans had three inches of snow.

Thus far the month of December had been tagged as the coldest on record the past several decades, as well as for the most snowfall.

Just his luck.

Coming south in winter was generally associated with warmer temps. But not this trip. This time was different on a number of counts.

When Victoria Colby-Camp had called Riley Porter into her office on Christmas Eve, he had known that the case would be different from any other she'd assigned him. He'd put aside his plans to go home to Kansas City and visit his folks.

There was no client in this situation—not a single, official *paying* client anyway. The parents of the children Von Cassidy and Trinity Barrett rescued mere days ago had called Victoria from the hospital in Alabama where they had been reunited with their children and implored her to use the assets of her agency to stop this human trafficking network.

In addition, Von had gotten a glimpse of a young woman, Tessa Woods, involved in the network who had gone missing almost six years ago. How many other missing teens and children would be rescued by infiltrating this organization?

Victoria had made a solemn promise to do all she could to make that happen.

The FBI in Chicago, New Orleans and Huntsville, Alabama, had formed a task force to get to the root of this evil network.

Right there in the hospital, on Christmas Eve, a preliminary strategy had been put into place. One of the captured kidnappers, Russell "Buzz" Smith, had spilled his guts hours earlier in hopes of a lighter sentence. He'd sworn that this had been his first job with the trafficking organization. He was relatively young and seriously scared and straight-up desperate enough to do whatever was asked of him.

With his cooperation an opportunity had presented itself. Since the names of those captured or fatally injured in the Huntsville showdown had not been released to the press at the time, it was entirely possible—as far as the public knew—that one of the bad guys had escaped.

The end result had placed the Colby Agency in a very unique situation. Riley was the right age and possessed the necessary coloring—brown hair and gold eyes—and build to pass himself off as Buzz Smith. Those who had met Buzz were either dead or being detained. No one else in the organization had seen Buzz face-to-face or spoken directly to him. He had been hired by one of the kidnappers who'd lost his life in the course of the operation.

Putting through a call to the contact provided by Buzz Smith had set an operation in motion. Posing as Buzz, Riley had been instructed by the contact to come to New Orleans and report all that he knew.

Riley sipped the whiskey he'd ordered an hour ago. He needed to fit in with the not-so-low-key crowd partying the night away in this rebuilt warehouse-turned-bar on the fringes of downtown New Orleans. But he couldn't risk dulling his awareness in any capacity, so he sipped the drink slowly and tipped the waitress whenever she stopped to ensure he stayed on her good side.

Riley had made the call less than twenty-four hours ago. This place—the Rusty Hinge, a sleazy bar way, way off Bourbon Street—had been named as the rendezvous point by the contact. Buzz Smith had sworn that he'd given up all the information provided to him in the way of a briefing when hired, basically just enough to get Riley in the door.

It would have to be enough.

With only a scumbag's word, Riley had arrived at the rendezvous location an hour early for the meeting with the network's contact. Riley had taken a position with his back to the wall at a table for two as far from the entrance of the Rusty Hinge as could be gotten. The weapon hidden in his waistband at the small of his back would be worthless if he wasn't prepared and on his toes. He set the nearly empty tumbler on the table and surveyed the crowd of after-Christmas revelers.

Any one of them could be watching him, waiting for an opportunity to take him out. Determination tightened his jaw. Considering the importance of his part in this operation, he wasn't afraid of dying, only of failure. This case was far too important to be put off for any reason. Every squandered minute could mean the loss of another child or teen. Riley couldn't waste a single moment, not even the time wasted in dying.

Two men swaggered through the front doors, the only entrance or exit for the establishment Riley had noticed in the public area. There would be one in the back somewhere. The fire code would never permit only one access route. He assumed the door marked Employees Only led to a stock area where another entrance must exist. So he'd been keeping an eye on the bar as well.

The newcomers inventoried the crowd, their gazes eventually settling on Riley's table. When they moved in his direction tension rippled through his muscles. This was it. One man was a head taller than the other. The shorter guy sported a shiny, bald head. Both wore heavy coats, likely concealing weapons.

Riley adjusted the ball cap he wore to ensure the two—if they were his contacts—understood he was the man they sought. The cap was red and sported a popular Alabama college football logo. Buzz Smith hailed from Alabama and wanted the world to know it.

Levi Stark, a colleague from the Colby Agency, and Special Agent Lee Ross from the local New Orleans Bureau office were in the vicinity for backup. But the success of this operation depended upon the two staying in the background. To that end, Riley was unaware of their exact locations except that they were nearby. Communication devices had been left out of the scenario due to the increased risk. They could take no unnecessary chances.

Tracking devices had been installed in Riley's boot heels. That was the extent of the precautions he could afford to take for the moment. But he wasn't worried.

Backup was close. He fully trusted both men to do their jobs. One of the two was likely stationed outside in preparation for efficient relocation if necessary. The other, the Bureau agent, was likely amid the crowd. Riley hadn't spotted him but if the agent was good at his job that was to be expected.

And Riley was highly trained to deal with the unexpected. His former career as a Navy SEAL ensured he was fully prepared to evade, outstrategize and outmaneuver the enemy as well as to operate in the midst of that same enemy.

A sense of mind-clearing calm settled over Riley as the two new arrivals stopped at his table; one eyed him with blatant suspicion, then with a quick look around, asked, "Smith?"

"You the man in charge?" Riley demanded with an arrogant thrust of his chin and without bothering to confirm his identity. "I don't want to talk to some peon." He leaned across the table showing no fear. "Somebody set us up. Now everyone else is dead. Whoever did this knew exactly what our movements would be. Knew everything." He shook his head. "I'm not trusting just anybody. I want to talk to the man in charge."

The two men exchanged a look.

Three, four beats passed.

"Seems like you got yourself an attitude, Mr. Smith. What makes you think," the shorter guy with the shiny head and a hawklike nose asked, "we care who you trust or what you think?"

"Or—" the first man who'd spoken leaned down and braced his palms on the tabletop to look Riley more closely in the eyes "—if you live or die?"

"Maybe—" Riley downed the last of his whiskey "—because you're here. And because you and your boss might want to consider that whoever set us up is damned smart. If he did it once, chances are he'll do it again. And until you know who *he* is, then you can't protect yourself. *Or* your operation."

"We don't need you to figure that out," the taller guy said with a smirk. *"Chances are,"* he mocked, indifference in his tone and in his eyes, "you won't be around long enough for it to matter to you one way or another." He straightened and hitched his head toward the door. "Let's go," he said to his buddy. "We're done here."

"Folks get nervous," Riley said, causing both to hesitate, "if they think there's a loose end hanging around." His gaze zeroed in on the one who appeared to be in charge, the taller one. "Makes 'em desperate. Desperation fuels panic. Next thing you know they make a mistake and give themselves away *before* they have a chance to get in the way—if you know what I mean, again. But then, maybe you've got the situation under control and aren't worried about anyone on the inside setting you up a second time."

The indifference in the man's narrow gaze shifted to uncertainty. "Outside. Now." He turned his back and cut through the crowd, his buddy following.

Riley had pushed all the right buttons. He scooted back his chair and stood. At least he had their attention. Taking his time, he pulled on his coat, then made a path through the crowd of bodies. The waitress smiled at him as he passed a table she was serving.

The instant the entry doors cracked open

the sharp sting of cold air greeted Riley. Damned cold. It wasn't supposed to be like this. Just his luck, he reflected for about the tenth time today.

Nature's white blanket still cloaked the landscape, drawing the light from the full moon. Even the bare limbs of the trees served as shelves for winter's unexpected gift, adding an eerie glow to the landscape.

Riley had taken a mere three steps away from the door when a muzzle nudged firmly into his back. "Keep walking," the owner of the weapon instructed. "All the way to the gray SUV on your left."

Hawk-nose. Riley didn't have to glance back, he recognized the gruff voice. The taller one was likely close by or in the SUV already. Riley followed the instructions, crossing the parking lot to the specified vehicle.

"Now what?" Riley asked, not about to make any aspect of this easy.

Hawk-nose patted him down, discovered the weapon and claimed it. "Get in."

Riley reached for the front passenger door.

"The back."

"Where we going?" Riley asked. "To the boss?"

"Just get in."

The muzzle burrowed deeper into Riley's coat, reminding him that his choices were limited for buying additional time for his backup to prepare for following. He opened the back passenger-side door and climbed in. As he'd presumed, the taller of the two sat behind the steering wheel.

"Take off your clothes," the driver ordered, his gaze on Riley via the rearview mirror.

Now there was one Riley hadn't expected. "Say what?"

"Take 'em off," he repeated and tossed a pair of gray coveralls over the seat.

Riley wasn't happy about it but he understood exactly what they were up to and it wasn't good. He had little choice but to comply. Getting inside this operation was the goal, whatever the risk.

Taking his time, he peeled off his coat, then the rest—including his boots. When he'd pulled on the coveralls he reached for his boots to tug them back on. There was snow on the ground after all.

"You won't need those," Hawk-nose, who still loomed in the open door, said. He snagged the boots as well as Riley's clothes.

"In case you hadn't noticed," Riley reminded the two, "it's cold as hell."

"Socks, too." Hawk-nose stuck his hand in front of Riley. "Hurry up. It's cold out here," he tacked on in a mocking tone.

Riley peeled off his socks and tossed them to the guy. "Anything else?" Not that he had anything else to fork over.

The rear door slammed shut in his face. Riley glanced at the guy in front of him, then swung his attention to the one outside. It was tough to see beyond the darkly tinted windows, but the clothes Riley had shed, boots included, were dumped between two parked cars. The boots were his favorite pair. Not to mention they carried the tracking device. Nothing he could do about that.

The hawk-nosed guy headed back to the SUV. He opened the rear passenger door. "Slide over." He gestured toward the other side of the seat with his weapon.

Riley scooted over and the other man

climbed in next to him. "Let's get out of here," he said to his buddy.

The driver started the engine. "I guess you're gonna get your wish, Mr. Smith. There's someone who wants to talk to you after all."

"As long as he's higher up the food chain," Riley said.

Hawk-nose rammed the muzzle of his handgun into Riley's temple. "Your mouth is going to get you killed. You should keep it closed for now if you want to keep breathing, pal."

Riley turned his face toward the man next to him, ignoring the business end of the gun. "I'm not your pal. I'm the guy who's going to provide you and your partner here with a little more job security."

Fury detonated in the man's eyes as the interior light faded to black. "I don't know why we can't kill him right now," he snarled.

"You make a mess in my SUV," the driver warned as the vehicle rolled out onto the deserted street, "and I'll kill *you*."

Hawk-nose wasn't put off by his colleague's threat. "I think he's bluffing," he mused. "Probably working with the cops."

Riley didn't flinch, didn't take his fierce glare off the man with the gun. The streetlights provided enough illumination for him to see that his scare tactics weren't working.

"He don't know nothing," Hawk-nose suggested. "If he's not working with the cops, he's just trying to get a promotion."

"The boss'll be the judge of that," the driver reminded his colleague.

That piece of news was what he had wanted to hear. Riley relaxed into the seat, directed his attention straight ahead.

He was in…at least far enough to get a face-to-face with the boss.

The first step. If he could convince the boss of his own usefulness, maybe—just maybe—he could get all the way into the organization.

It was the only way to dismantle an operation this large and this sophisticated.

From the inside.

He would, as quickly as possible, learn the key players and then he would move on to step two. That was the most time sensitive and crucial step: take out one or more pivotal pieces of the foundation. Then the entire network collapsed.

Step two would be easy as long as he stayed alive.

Chapter Two

11:05 p.m.

The cold wind whistled through the cracks in the window frame. Tessa touched the wood frame, registering the roughness of the peeling paint that had once been white and the chunks of missing caulk that allowed the frigid air to seep into the room.

Her gaze drifted past the wavy glass of the century-old window, past the intimidating black iron bars, to the snow that remained on the ground. She couldn't remember the last time it had snowed for Christmas. Her lips ached with the need to smile. But smiling was forbidden.

The Master did not allow his family to smile or to laugh.

Holidays were difficult sometimes.

Memories crept in…reminding her of how it used to be.

Before…

"Tessa."

A tremble slid through her, shaking her bones. She turned to face him. "Yes?"

"Ensure the children and the patients remain in their rooms."

For a long moment she simply stared in response. Taller than most men, six-three or -four. He worked out religiously to keep his muscles big and hard. Used steroids liberally to be sure they stayed that way well after his youth had become a distant memory. Always dressed in elegant attire. Everything about him, except his skin, was black. Hair, eyes, clothing. He used his coloring, his size and even his clothes to inspire fear.

It always worked.

No one dared cross him.

"Tessa?"

The warning in his tone trapped the oxygen beneath her sternum for a moment more. "Yes." She blinked, forced away all other thought save his order. "I'll make sure."

He surveyed her room, no doubt noting that the covers of her bed had not as of yet been turned down. "I believe it's past your bedtime, is it not?"

Tessa nodded. She smoothed a hand over the pink flannel of her gown. The metal key in the pocket pressed reassuringly against her hip. "I was about to lie down, but I thought I heard something outside."

"That would be security's concern."

"Of course."

She held her breath until he'd gone. As long as she obeyed, she could take care of the children and the patients. More caution was necessary. She couldn't make a mistake. For years she had watched the unthinkable treatment of those confined...she had worked diligently to reach a position of some authority so that she could change that sadness. So that she could devise a plan.

No matter the cost to her, she could not lose that small power.

In spite of that need, she still longed for freedom...escape. There had been opportunities...few and rare, but opportunities nonetheless. She would not take advantage of the chance to escape without being able to take the others with her.

To take *the* child.

An ache rose in her throat.

No matter the cost.

Pay attention. She squared her shoulders. Something was happening tonight. There was an unusual tension in the air. A sense of anticipation.

For the past hour or so she had seen the seemingly frantic coming and going of the others assigned to the house. There were no other deliveries or pick-ups on the schedule for the next eight days.

Fear trickled into her veins. If he had increased his schedule… No. She shook her head. It was too risky. He wouldn't do that. She would know if changes had been set in motion.

Taking a deep, steadying breath, Tessa turned away from the window and moved toward the door, her bare feet soundless on the frigid floor.

She couldn't think about the deliveries or the pick-ups. Taking care of the children and the patients was all that mattered. That was her life now.

At least until the time was right. The opportunity was close...so very close.

A shiver rumbled through her body as defeat weighed heavily down upon her. *Stop.* Nothing would stop her...she would find a way, no matter the obstacles that arose. Her plan was solid...but the timing had to be perfect.

Outside her door, along the dark, silent corridor were two large rooms besides her own. Tessa removed the key from her pocket and unlocked the first door.

She didn't turn on the light for fear of waking the sleeping children. Whatever was happening, it could be dangerous. The children would be safest if they were asleep. Noise—not even a whimper—was allowed past eight in the evening.

Tessa crouched down next to the first bed. She pinched her lips together to prevent the forbidden. The urge to sweep soft blond hair back from the little girl's forehead forced her to clench her fingers. She drew the fist to her lips and resisted the new urge to cry.

She had to protect *the* child.

She had to protect them all.

In a few days, at most, everything would change…it would all be over.

Clinging to that hope, Tessa moved to the next bed, then the next and the next. All four children slept soundly. All beautiful blond-haired girls with dazzling blue eyes.

And one, her gaze wandered back to the first bed, was the most beautiful of all.

Careful not to make any noise, she padded back to the door. Once in the corridor she closed and locked the door to the children's room.

Her heart sank into her belly as she approached the next door. Tessa moistened her lips and unlocked it. Her hand shook as she removed the key and slid it into her pocket. Bracing for the misery, she turned the knob. A creak made her flinch. She prayed those inside, too, would be asleep. It would be best if they didn't ask questions. Their cries and pleas took a heavy toll on Tessa.

Holding her breath, she eased into the dark room. The thick drapes on the windows blocked the moonlight from filtering inside. Beyond the drapes, on all the windows in the house, were iron bars that prevented anything inside from slipping out.

She moved quickly to the first of four narrow beds that lined the walls. Like the children, the women slept soundly. With no nightlight, Tessa couldn't see their faces in the thick blackness, but she could hear their breathing. Slow, deep, rhythmic. Sleep was their only escape from a reality too horrifying to endure for more than a few hours at a time.

Please let me be able to help them before it's too late.

The distinct sense of urgency thick in the room caused Tessa's stomach to tighten with emotion.

Time was running out.

She had to be ready to act. She couldn't allow this to happen *again*.

Her plan had to work.

Determination chasing away the uncertainty and fear edging out her courage, she turned and walked quietly back across the room, then as noiselessly as possible she exited and locked the door.

Let them sleep. Reality would intrude soon enough.

The corridor was quiet. Tessa hesitated outside her own room. She should go to bed. But sleep would be impossible. As the time drew nearer, the anticipation built, preventing sleep and prompting a restlessness that wouldn't go away.

She bit her lower lip and considered the risk involved with indulging her curiosity.

Learning what tonight's unusual activities were about could prove useful to her plan…but if he caught her she would be punished severely.

No one defied the Master.

Tessa inhaled a breath of courage and set one bare foot in front of the other; her destination: the landing. Each step frayed her nerves a little more. This house was so very old…the floors creaked. It had taken her months to learn the best places to step to avoid the loudest groans.

She didn't release the air in her lungs until she reached the landing. Repeating a silent mantra for protection, she dared to lean over the railing just far enough to view the stairs that wound down to the second, then the first floor.

Clear.

Holding her breath, she glanced upward to the fourth floor—*his floor*. No one was allowed up there unless personally invited by the Master.

Her gaze dropped back to the stairs winding downward. Whatever was going on, the trouble had apparently settled in the questioning room.

Another shudder rattled her bones as she considered that room…the basement.

He'd turned it into a chamber of horrors. Steel bars had been erected at both ends of the massive area for using as cells. Every square foot of the floor space between acted as a stage for terror.

Torture devices.

Tessa closed her eyes and summoned her fleeing courage yet again. The silence closed in on her, crumbling away at her fragile bravado.

Just go.

Blocking the warning voices inside her head, she descended quickly to the second floor. She hesitated on the landing. More of that consuming silence. The soldiers who used the second floor for sleeping quarters were either rallied for whatever was going on or adjourned to their rooms. It was past curfew, but until a short time ago there had been much coming and going. That she could not be certain of their status made her decision to get a closer look at what was happening even riskier.

Had the Master summoned his entire team for some impromptu action?

Perhaps the police had finally discovered his identity and this hidden compound. Tessa had prayed for years that the police would come, that somehow she and the others would be rescued.

But *he* was too smart for the police. Eventually she had realized that no one was coming. There would be no savior... no rescue.

Unless she stepped into the role and organized her own rescue.

The first floor proved equally quiet. She made her way from room to room and from window to window, using her memory as her guide since she didn't dare turn on any lights. Her breath hitched when two dark figures moved past a rear window. The perimeter guards. Two men walked the grounds twenty-four/seven. The Master never relied solely on security cameras or other gadgets.

So…whatever was happening was in the questioning room. Her gaze lowered to the wood floor. She moistened her lips and swallowed back the confirming lump of fear that had lodged in her throat.

Trouble.

Someone had either been identified as a potential informant or an enemy had been captured. Only once since she'd been with him had an informant been uncovered. He had forced her to watch the slow, agonizing torture and ultimate murder of the man.

Two other times an enemy had been brought here. Most of the time anyone presumed to be the enemy was simply killed on the spot. But if there was information to be gained, the enemy was interrogated. Always here. Always mercilessly.

Tessa returned to the wide entry hall and held her breath. She listened, straining with the effort. Silence. They had to be in the questioning room. That level had been meticulously insulated to ensure no sound escaped or invaded the space.

The original entry point had been in the hall, but the Master had long ago closed that access and created a hidden entrance in his library.

Directly across the entry hall from the parlor, the library had provided hours of escape for her in the beginning. It had taken almost a year for her to accept her new lot in life, then she had turned her attention to gaining trust and responsibility. One day, those years of planning and praying would provide freedom.

Inside the library, bookshelves lined the walls, floor to ceiling. A massive desk sat in the middle of the room, flanked by four chairs. This was where he held his strategy sessions. Only recently had she been allowed to attend the sessions. She had not gained a chair as of yet, but she was allowed to sit on the floor in one corner. A trusted member of the family was assigned a corner and eventually a chair.

A section of the shelving, four feet wide and nine feet tall opened, revealing a wide staircase that led down to the questioning room—or dungeon as she preferred to call it.

There would be only one place she could hide from view and that was about one-third of the way down. She would be able to see around the wall that ended at that point while still concealing her presence— if no one stood at the bottom of the stairs or happened to be coming up as she started down.

She removed the book that concealed the button, then pressed. The section of shelving with its faux books slowly, quietly moved open via its hydraulic hinges. Raised voices vibrated on the cool air. The temperature down there was kept at a steady sixty degrees, adding to the discomfort of those imprisoned and/or being interrogated.

The instant Tessa moved down to the first step she pressed the closing mechanism. The door crept closed behind her. She shivered, as much from the cold as from the fear.

She stood very still and listened.

The Master and his two deputies were

grilling a fourth man. Tessa didn't recognize his voice. She needed to see. She bit the inside of her jaw and considered whether she dared.

The timing was too close to her plans to ignore the situation. If operations or schedules were about to change related to the capture of an informant or an enemy, she needed to be aware.

Easing forward, she peeked around the wall. A man wearing gray coveralls was secured to the interrogation chair. Her heart bumped her chest. His face already showed signs of torture. The Master stood back and watched as his deputies, Brooks and Howard, questioned the man. The man looked young. Brown hair. Definitely no one she had seen before.

She waited a moment more for her heart to stop pounding, then she moved.

Without daring to take a breath she descended the steps and moved around to hide beneath the stairs. Supply containers provided cover for her crouched position. She willed her heart to slow once more, thanked God the fabric of her gown hadn't so much as whispered against her skin.

She inhaled slowly, soundlessly until her breathing returned to normal.

She wrapped her arms around her knees and maintained her balance on the pads of her feet. They called the man "Smith." Tessa knew no one named Smith.

"Considering your fear of capture," the Master said, his deputies falling silent as he spoke, "why make contact with us? Why not go into hiding?"

Smith stared up at the Master as if he had no fear at all. Tessa's eyes widened in expectation of retaliation.

"I had no place else to go," he said with no humility whatsoever. "That's why I took this job in the first place. I'd run out of other options."

Brooks, the taller of the two deputies, backhanded Smith, almost toppling the chair.

"You believe," the Master went on, "that we have an obligation to take you in?" He laughed, that deep ugly sound that haunted Tessa's dreams far too often. "This is no halfway house, Mr. Smith. In fact, in your case, it's the end of the line."

The Master turned and started toward the stairs. Tessa held her breath.

"Finish this," the Master ordered, "and feed him to the alligators."

Howard, the bald man with the big nose, who leered at her whenever the Master wasn't looking, chuckled. "Guess you aren't as smart as you thought, Mr. Smith."

"I'm smart enough to know when I've grown overconfident. Maybe your Master would be better served to recognize that in himself."

Silence fell over the room. The Master paused before reaching the stairs and turned to face the man who dared to challenge him.

"Your soldier, Kennamer, liked to brag about how you're fearless," Smith continued. "How you're untouchable." He shrugged. "Seems funny to me that if that's the case, you just had a major operation go south on you. But then," Smith added, "maybe that's why he also bragged that your god complex would be your downfall."

A moment, then two, of thick silence.

Tessa's heart stumbled to a near stop.

"Can we kill him now?" Brooks suggested.

More of that heavy silence.

"Perhaps not just yet," the Master said.

Surprise flared beneath Tessa's breast. The Master never showed mercy like this. Did he fear that Smith was right? She gave her head a little shake. Impossible.

"Perhaps," the Master went on, stepping back toward Smith, "we'll interrogate Mr. Smith once more after we've all had some rest. We'll have a fresh perspective then."

Tessa tilted her head back and watched the Master climb the stairs. If he checked her room and found her missing… No, stop, he wouldn't. He trusted her to do as she was told after so many years.

Howard kicked Smith's chair and cursed about the missed opportunity to feed the pets.

Tessa shivered at the thought of the swamp surrounding this awful place. Howard and Brooks fed the gators regularly to ensure the beasts considered the area a generous feeding ground. Anyone who stumbled onto the property would likely never make it even close enough to enter the electronic surveillance field.

The whole compound was off the grid. No landlines for communications. Even the power was provided by a massive generator. And the water was obtained from the property and directed into the house via a state-of-the-art filtration system.

Tessa doubted there was more than a dozen people who even knew of their existence deep in the wooded swampland outside New Orleans.

But now someone did…this man, *Smith*. He knew. He was here and still alive.

Anticipation fired through her as Brooks and Howard stomped up the stairs. The overhead lights extinguished, leaving the room in almost total darkness. Only the dim lights from the electronic equipment provided minuscule illumination.

Did she dare question this Smith herself? Could he possibly possess information that would help her? Hope bloomed despite the years of desolation that had left her soul barren.

Smith would die in a few hours. That was a certainty.

He presented no peril to her.

Still…he could tell the Master that she'd come down here.

"Are you going to come out now?"

The air in Tessa's lungs evacuated.

"They're gone," Smith said.

He'd seen her sneak down the stairs!

She chewed her bottom lip. Would he assume he'd been hallucinating if she didn't move and didn't say a word?

"I know you're there," he murmured, his voice weaker now. "You might as well come out." He made a muffled sound, like a laugh. "I'm obviously in no position to do you harm."

But getting caught talking to him could get her killed.

Tessa couldn't bear to think what would happen to the child then.

That familiar ache of fear sliced through her.

"I could use a drink of water."

Tessa blinked away the terrifying thoughts.

"Please."

The desperation in his plea touched her heart…but he was one of them.

A man who earned money by stealing children.

She couldn't trust him.

Defeat pressed in on her.

She couldn't trust anyone.

Chapter Three

As much as the desperate urge to escape clawed at him, Riley's fascination with the girl—no, the woman—staring wide-eyed at him held his full attention.

This was Tessa Woods.

He'd carefully reviewed her file. Studied the photos of the sweet seventeen-year-old with the silky blond hair and huge blue eyes. Her friends and family had labeled her sweet and kind. Intelligent and earnest. But naive and far too trusting.

Was that why nearly six years later she was still alive?

Or had she been brainwashed into becoming as ruthless as those who'd taken her while on a high school senior class trip only a few miles from her small hometown in Mississippi?

The well-worn, pink flannel gown fell loosely around her but as she'd moved toward him the soft-looking fabric had molded to her slim frame. He wanted to tell her how desperately her family had searched for her all these years. How they even now held out hope that she would return to them.

But Tessa Woods was twenty-three years old now. Chances were she was not the sweet, naive young girl she'd been when abducted by these bastards.

"Just a drink of water," he murmured, careful to keep his voice low and unthreatening. "That's all I'm asking," he assured her, when in truth he was asking for the world. That she would help him bring down this operation...that she would be unchanged.

She reached up. He tensed. Slender fingers brushed her hair behind her right ear.

As slowly and thoughtfully as she'd approached him, she turned and padded barefoot across the room. He'd already inventoried the array of torture devices. There was an electrical shock station, one for water boarding and what appeared to be a carving area. Lots of box cutters and knives.

Just the sort of place a guy wanted to end up.

The woman he was convinced was Tessa Woods picked up a large beaker from the water-torture area and held it beneath the faucet. She glanced at the staircase before turning on the faucet just long enough to run a few ounces of water. Then she moved toward him once more. She was nervous. She checked the stairs twice crossing the room. Whatever her position in the organization, she obviously wasn't supposed to be down here.

Standing before him, she hesitated before extending the beaker to his mouth. She kept her gaze on his mouth as she tilted the beaker. He watched her face, assessing her trepidation. She was definitely scared. Of him, of being caught. Maybe of the truth.

Did she remember her life before? Or had these lowlifes ensured that history was buried so deeply that she wouldn't ever recall? Victoria Colby-Camp had told him of how her son had been brainwashed in just such a way. His memories had been twisted to the point that he had firmly believed his parents hadn't loved him and had abandoned him. Had this woman suffered the same?

The water trickled down his chin. She drew the beaker away and he licked the dampness. Holding the glass container with both hands, she dared to meet his eyes.

"Who are you?"

His chest contracted at the sound of her voice—gentle, quiet, filled with tentative wonder. "Russell Smith. And you?"

She chewed her lip a moment before answering. "Tessa."

Anticipation detonated deep inside him. "Tessa what?"

Another hesitation, this one far longer than the first. "Just Tessa." Uncertainty flashed in her eyes before she looked away. "Why are you here?"

The urge to tell her he was here to rescue her, to stop these bastards, nearly overwhelmed him. But he couldn't take the risk. For all he knew at this point, she could be one of them.

"I'm here to help," he hedged, choosing his words carefully.

"You're a new soldier?" She didn't bother looking away this time, allowing him to see the disappointment tinged with anger in her eyes. The same emotions that altered the pitch of her voice ever so slightly.

He shrugged. "Maybe."

Her fingers visibly tightened on the beaker. "Why are they interrogating you?"

"Isn't that routine?" His jaw throbbed from the punches the two goons had taken turns throwing. "Don't they do this to every new recruit?"

She moved her head side to side. "Only the ones who double-cross them or try to hamper their efforts."

"What about you?" he ventured. "Are you a soldier?"

Another shake of her head.

"Daughter?" He searched her face for a tell-tale emotional reaction. The guy who called himself the Master was old enough to be her father. But Riley knew better. This was Tessa Woods. "Wife?"

Her shoulders lifted then fell. "I belong to the Master."

Indignation knotted in his gut. This was going to be every bit as sick as he'd suspected. "The *Master?*" He knew very well who she meant. The bastard in charge. He hadn't given his name. The two who'd brought Riley here, and then used him as a punching bag, had only referred to their boss as "Master." "He doesn't have a name?"

"We're forbidden to speak it." She turned away from him and returned the beaker to its place.

The way she took pains to see that it was placed exactly as she'd found it warned again that she feared being discovered, now or later, down here with him. That she dared to take the risk suggested one of two things. Either the Master hoped her innocence would draw out the truth or she was in the market for help.

Too soon to tell.

What he needed was time.

Unfortunately that was a luxury he didn't have. The Master and his henchmen hadn't completely bought his story so far and there was a very great likelihood that in a few hours he would be a dead man.

"Tessa?"

That he called her by name appeared to startle her.

"Any chance you could cut me loose?" He shrugged. "If they're just going to kill me, I'd rather miss that part."

Her gaze drifted to the stairs again, before settling on his. "Tell them Renwick was responsible for the ambush. That he sent you, but you're willing to negotiate your alliance."

Talk about surprised. Here he'd thought the lady was this innocent little angel but she was talking ambushes and negotiations. "And that's supposed to keep me alive?" Oh, yeah, he could definitely see how admitting that the enemy had sent him would do the trick.

"His people recruited you." She thought for a moment. "Phipps. Tall, thin, red hair. He offered you a hundred thousand to set up a takedown. You never met Renwick. Only Phipps."

"Telling them that I'm a mole doesn't seem like a good plan to me." His wrists were burning from the tightness of the ropes but that was the least of his problems at the moment.

Those big blue eyes stared right through him, as if she hoped to penetrate his brain and make him pay attention. "It's a good plan."

She turned and started for the stairs.

"Maybe I'll just take my chances with the truth." Might as well cover all the bases... just in case.

Tessa paused at the bottom of the stairs and met his gaze once more. "Then you'll die."

TESSA CHECKED THE SECURITY peephole before activating the latch to enter the library. She held her breath until she confirmed that there was no one in the room.

The pressure of the air seemed to change as she closed the door leading to the basement and held still to listen. The silence continued to linger in the air.

Counting him, there had only been three people in the questioning room and two patrolling the grounds.

If the others were in their rooms for the

night, she should be able to reach her room without incident.

She checked the entry hall before leaving the library. The house was completely dark but she knew every square foot. Learning the furniture placement had ensured she never bumped into a table or chair. The slightest noise would bring trouble.

A loud thump echoed. Tessa froze. Outside, she determined. Another solid thump.

Car doors.

She hurried to the nearest window. Two SUVs had arrived. Five, six, seven…she counted seven men loitering around the vehicles.

The soldiers.

This was downtime. No ongoing operations. Two of the patients were ready for delivery. Risks weren't taken during this time.

Had the arrival of the man downstairs, Smith, generated all this activity?

"Tessa."

Her blood froze in her veins. *Turn around. Face him.* She knew better than to ignore him even for a second.

She faced him. "Yes?" Her mind spun with usable excuses for why she was not in her room. The key in her pocket seemed to burn her skin through the flannel.

He allowed her to carry a key. One key that fit the lock to the children's room and that of the patients as well as her own room. If she angered him, he would take the privilege from her.

"What're you doing down here?" He turned on a table lamp and assessed her for several seconds. "You should be asleep by now."

"Everyone else is asleep. The doors slamming outside woke me. I was worried." She gestured to the window. "Is something wrong?" Her voice sounded a little shaky. She prayed he wouldn't make something of it.

"There's nothing for you to worry about." He motioned for her to come to him. "Your attention is needed elsewhere."

Tessa moved close enough for him to take her arm. The feel of his hand on her skin made her sick to her stomach. "I guess I'm a little anxious after what happened in Alabama."

"A nuisance." He guided her to the stairs. "Nothing more. No need to fret."

She nodded. "Sorry. I wasn't thinking."

"It's a busy time," he offered with uncharacteristic understanding. "I'll expect you to be well rested in the morning."

Her head moved up and down of its own accord, proof of her comprehension of his advisement. That he seemed unfazed by her forbidden action made her all the more nervous. She forced one foot above the other, climbing the stairs without looking back and hoping that would be the end of it.

"Tessa."

Fear swirled wildly in her belly. She turned back, keeping her hand planted firmly on the railing, her feet braced to run. "Yes."

"Do not mistake my indulgence of your behavior tonight for a softening of the rules." He pressed her with a harsh gaze. "You know the rules. I will not tolerate another infraction. Not even from you."

"I understand."

Turning her back to him and climbing the remainder of the stairs was the hardest thing she had done in a long time. She had taken a major risk coming downstairs after curfew.

If he discovered just how far she'd gone in breaking the rules Mr. Smith wouldn't be the only one dying tomorrow.

Chapter Four

Chicago, Sunday, December 27, 7:00 a.m.

Victoria Colby-Camp poured another cup of coffee and held it tightly in both hands. She needed the warmth. The city remained blanketed in snow, but that wasn't the reason she felt chilled to the bone.

Eight hours had passed with no contact from Riley Porter. Levi Stark, another of her investigators, and FBI Special Agent Lee Ross had lost visual contact on Riley before midnight. The tracking devices had been dumped in the parking lot of the rendezvous location.

There had been no word since that revelation.

Victoria had not slept in the same. Finally at six this morning she had joined her son, Jim, here at the office. There was little she could do, other than pray, but just being here made her feel more involved.

Words could not adequately describe the relief Victoria felt at her agency's accomplishment over the holiday weekend. Sixteen children had been recovered. But the recovery had not stopped this ruthless organization.

She exhaled a heavy breath and moved across the lounge to peer out the window. Daylight had crept across the snow-laden streets, but the sun remained veiled by the heavy clouds. More snow was on the way.

She thought about the file on Tessa Woods the Bureau had provided. The Bureau contacts in Mississippi had insisted on notifying the family. Victoria had considered the move a mistake despite the fact that Von Cassidy, a trusted Colby Agency investigator, had been nearly certain the blonde woman she'd encountered had been Tessa Woods. There was still a chance it wasn't her.

No matter. Julia and Warren Woods, the parents, had already contacted Victoria.

The telephone conversation had been emotionally excruciating. Von had agreed to meet with the parents and answer any questions. The parents had flown to Nashville. Von and Trinity Barrett had left their Gatlinburg getaway long enough to make the trip to Nashville. Like Von, the parents were convinced that the blonde woman was indeed their daughter.

Riley Porter's mission was to find a way to bring down the organization and to recover Tessa Woods, as well as any other victims.

Worry twisted in Victoria's chest. She pushed it away and lifted her chin in defiance of the nagging doubts. Riley was highly trained. As a Navy SEAL he had rescued hostages and colleagues amid far more treacherous conditions. Victoria had complete faith in him.

"Mother."

A smile lifted the corners of Victoria's lips. Her heart still fluttered when her son called her Mother. She turned to him. "Any news?"

Jim freshened his coffee, then shook his head. "Not yet. Agent Ross and his team have begun a discreet search. Our man Stark is working on an avenue of his own."

Levi Stark was another outstanding Colby investigator. If he had a lead of his own, Victoria felt confident it would prove worthwhile.

"Any word from the task force?" she asked, hoping Jim had heard something she hadn't.

He shook his head. "But," he qualified, "with the number of great and determined minds we have working on this case, I'm certain we'll have a break soon."

Victoria nodded. The Bureau here in Chicago, in Huntsville, Alabama, as well as in New Orleans, had formed a task force to stop this ruthless ring of bastards.

It couldn't happen fast enough to suit Victoria.

"I saw on your desk calendar that you have an appointment with your doctor next week."

"Just a routine physical," Victoria assured her son. "I'm a few months behind. My doctor isn't too happy with me." She sipped her coffee. "But I've been a little busy lately."

Judging by Jim's expression, he wasn't going to let it go quite so lightly. "Keep the appointment. I don't want you ignoring your health."

A smile widened no matter that she knew he was very serious. "I will keep the appointment. My health is important. I have two beautiful grandchildren who need me."

Jim's gaze locked with hers. "*I* need you."

Emotion expanded in Victoria's chest. "Well." She took a much-needed breath. "How are the negotiations going with your buyer for the Equalizer shop?"

"He's willing to pay above asking price." Jim shrugged, his expression puzzled.

"You're not happy about that?" Seemed to Victoria that above asking price would be the optimum desirable situation. Particularly in this economy.

"We're this deep into negotiations," Jim explained, "and he still refuses to reveal his identity. His attorney claims the man just wants to maintain his anonymity. That he's a philanthropist and intends to use the Equalizers as a way to help those in need, particularly those who don't have the financial resources to help themselves."

Now she understood his unease. "Sounds too good to be true."

Jim nodded. "You know the adage. Whenever something sounds too good to be true, it usually is."

Victoria hoped that the idea that Tessa Woods was still alive wasn't too good to be true as well.

Chapter Five

New Orleans, 8:25 a.m.

This was going to hurt.

Wrists bound above his head and feet swinging several inches above the concrete floor, Riley braced for the coming pain.

Brooks shoved the paddle against Riley's abdomen. Electricity roared through his body. His muscles convulsed. His teeth clenched.

"You still sticking to your story?" Brooks demanded. "Don't have anything else to share?"

Riley struggled to catch his breath. "I've told you all there is to tell." His muscles burned. His shoulders throbbed with the effort of supporting his full body weight. His jaws ached from clenching his teeth.

"I just want to keep my job and stay out of prison."

Brooks thrust the paddle at him again.

Riley's body shuddered. Fire seemed to ignite across his skin. His stomach clenched.

"Just kill him and get it over with," Howard suggested. "This is a waste of time."

Brooks laughed. "I'm not done yet." He reached toward Riley once more.

"Wait!" Riley heaved a halting breath. "Wait," he muttered.

The smile on Brooks's face spread into a spiteful grin. "I thought you might change your mind."

Riley had held up through more than an hour of physical torture. He could have tolerated more, but the end result would have been the same. Death. These guys had no intention of allowing him to stay alive.

He had nothing to lose by going with Tessa's suggestion. If it was a setup, made no difference. At this point he was dead anyway.

"Renwick was behind the ambush in Alabama," Riley muttered. The aftereffects of the shock treatments were making his body tremble. "He tipped off the feds. One of the feds passed along the tip to a friend in Chicago."

"What friend in Chicago?" Howard demanded, skeptical.

Riley lolled his head back long enough to draw in a deep breath, then met the man's gaze. "I don't know. Some P.I. Doesn't matter. It's the feds that's on your back now. Renwick thought they would take down your organization. He was ticked off when the operation failed. He wants to be number one."

Brooks made a slow circle around Riley. "What do you know about Renwick?"

Riley didn't have a lot to go on. He'd just have to wing it. "I know he wants you and your boss to go down. That's what I know."

Howard and Brooks blasted the air with expletives, then Howard said, "You think telling us this is going to save your butt?"

Well, so much for that plan. "Do what you gotta do, man," Riley said, feigning defeat. "I'm telling you that the feds are the least of your problems. Renwick is hell-bent on coming out on top, which means you have to go down."

"If that bastard knows what's good for him," Brooks snarled, "he'd better stay in his own territory."

Riley licked his cracked lips, tasted the blood. His jaw wasn't broken but it had taken another beating. "I think he's planning a takeover of your territory." That was a shot in the dark. Judging by the fury that claimed both men's faces, he'd hit the target.

"The SOB has a death wish," Howard growled. He eyed Riley a long moment. "What exactly were Renwick's orders? I can't see him trusting an operation this big to one guy. Especially one like you."

"My job was to get in," Riley said. "Get the layout of your headquarters and find out what you had on the schedule for the next couple of weeks."

"Too bad—" Howard moved in close to Riley "—you failed."

Riley breathed a chuckle. "Two out of three ain't bad."

The muzzle of a weapon bored into the soft underside of his chin. "How," Brooks asked, his voice riddled with anger and scorn, "are you supposed to pass along information? Is there a tracking device?" He sneered. "I know you don't want us to start searching the only logical places."

Riley definitely wasn't game for a cavity search. "He knows what you lost in the ambush and that I'm in New Orleans to make contact. That's it."

Howard shook his head at his pal. "He's lying. No way Renwick sent him to us without a tracking device." He shifted his attention to Riley. "All we have to do is find it."

"I swear," Riley urged, "the only tracking device I had was in the heels of my boots. You dumped those last night, with the rest of my clothes, in the parking lot at that bar."

"Get the Master."

Howard glared at Brooks. "We can handle this."

Brooks shook his head. "Get him. Now."

Howard glared a bit longer at the man who was obviously his superior before following the order. Riley relaxed as best he could considering he hung like a side of beef from the hook in the ceiling.

Tessa had given him an out. What did that mean? Was she truly a captive? Even after all these years? Had she intended to help him? Maybe this whole thing was a sham of some kind. A game she had initiated. Who knew how warped her mind might be after spending nearly half a dozen years with these sickos.

Brooks crossed his arms and stared at Riley. Riley ignored him. Instead, he focused on what he needed to accomplish his mission. The Master's identity. If no one called or knew his name, then a DNA sample would be necessary—assuming he was in the system. Prints might serve the purpose. Riley needed as much information about the organization's operation as possible. Tessa may or may not have some knowledge of how things worked.

And he needed to get her and any other captives away from here.

Away from the lunatic who called himself the Master.

Footfalls on the stairs drew Riley's attention there.

"Now we'll see how much longer you'll keep breathing," Brooks warned.

The Master, wearing his high-class designer suit, descended the final step. He studied Riley for a time before moving toward him.

He stopped a few feet away. "Renwick sent you, did he?"

Riley's tension ratcheted a little higher. "Yes." He infused all the humility and desperation he could summon into the single word.

"How is my old friend Renwick?"

Trick question. "I wouldn't know," Riley said, suppressing a grimace. His hands and arms had gone completely numb. "My only contact was with Phipps." He looked the Master straight in the eyes. "You know, tall, thin guy with red hair. He provided my orders."

"Which were," the Master pressed.

"To infiltrate your organization and gather intelligence about your upcoming operations."

The silence that followed had Riley holding his breath.

"Was that the extent of your orders?" Masters demanded.

"I can't tell you what was said word for word," Riley confessed. "If there's anything else, I can't call it to mind just now." He glanced up at his bound hands. "This isn't exactly conducive to brain power."

"We should just gut 'em," Howard suggested. "He's a waste of time."

The Master stared at the much shorter man until he visibly cowered, before shifting his attention back to Riley. "Cut him down."

Brooks and Howard exchanged a look of surprise. "What're we doing with him?" Brooks wanted to know.

"I haven't decided," the Master said as he returned to the staircase. He paused before taking the first step. "Feed him and get him properly attired."

The man in charge climbed the stairs, leaving Riley in the capable hands of his colleagues. Just his luck.

"This makes no sense," Howard growled. He glared at Riley. "I think you're bluffing."

Riley didn't bother arguing with him.

"Cut him down," Brooks snapped. "That's what the Master said."

Howard grumbled the entire time but he did as he was told. He climbed onto a step-ladder and cut the ropes. Riley attempted to land on his feet but his knees buckled and he crumpled to the floor.

Howard kicked him. "Get up."

When Riley had gotten to his feet, Howard shoved him toward the stairs. Brooks had already taken that route. As Riley climbed the steps the circulation returned to his arms, but his hands were still tightly bound and totally numb.

At the top of the stairs, Howard pushed him to the left and to another staircase. "Up," he ordered.

Riley climbed to the second floor. He took in as many of the details as possible in the short time it took to reach the door Howard directed him to. Long corridor, five doors. He hadn't encountered anyone else. Riley wondered where Tessa was. And why she'd decided to help him.

Every action was propelled by a motive. What was hers?

Howard opened the door and shoved

him into the room. "Take a shower. You stink."

Riley held out his bound hands. "Be kind of hard to do."

Howard pulled out his pocketknife and cut the bindings, then palmed his weapon. "Make one wrong move," he cautioned, while Riley rubbed at his wrists, "and I will kill you." Then he slammed the door, leaving Riley alone in the large bathroom.

Serviceable fixtures. Clean enough. He grabbed a towel from the shelf and slung it over the shower curtain rod and turned on the tap. A glance in the mirror confirmed that he had a swollen jaw, black eye and more than one split in his lips. He shook it off, refusing to let the pain steal his focus.

Once the coveralls were off, he kicked them aside and climbed into the shower.

He stood for a while with the warm water washing over his sore face and shoulders. There were no answers for additional questions. Whatever this Master had in mind for him, Riley had given him all he had. All Tessa had given him. But he had bought some time.

In an operation like this, that was the most he could hope for. To survive, minute by minute, hour by hour.

Riley took his time. No need to rush fate.

When the water had turned cold he shut it off and dragged back the curtain. He grabbed the towel and carefully dabbed his face before stepping out onto the cool tile floor.

His gaze locked with blue eyes.

Tessa.

He lowered the towel to cover himself.

She extended a neatly folded stack of clothing, hiking boots on top, toward him. "These are for you."

It took a second or two for him to regain his voice. "Thank you." He accepted the clothes.

"When you're dressed," she said, openly surveying his body, "you're to come to the kitchen."

"All right."

Her gaze bumped into his once more. "They'll be waiting there."

She left the room, closed the door behind her.

Strange. He shook his head and dried his skin. The situation grew more bizarre by the moment. For the first time in his life he could truthfully say he had no idea what to expect next.

The jeans and pullover crewneck shirt fit as if he'd bought them himself. Socks, hiking boots. Boots were a little loose, but not enough to matter. He ran his fingers through his damp hair and reached for the door.

Howard wasn't waiting in the corridor as Riley had expected. Apparently security was tight enough that no one was worried about him taking off or making any problematic moves.

Downstairs, the entry hall was deserted as well. Riley noted the high-tech keypad on the wall next to the front door. Definitely state-of-the-art security. This guy had no reason to worry about him escaping. Riley wasn't going anywhere until his hosts were ready for him to go.

Preferably not feet first.

Brooks stepped from a room beyond the library-like room they'd used for accessing the basement. Brooks jerked his head toward the door he'd exited, and then turned and walked back into the room.

That was his cue, Riley supposed.

The room where Brooks waited was the kitchen. Large. The usual amenities including an extra-long dining table with seating for twelve.

"Sit," Howard ordered, hitching his thumb toward the table.

A plate heaped with eggs, bacon and toast waited for him. Riley took the seat and reached first for the steaming cup of coffee.

Howard and Brooks stood near the door and waited without saying a word.

Riley ate. If the food was poisoned he was done for. He hadn't realized how hungry he was until he smelled the bacon. His body reacted to the fuel. Energy reviving his aching muscles.

When he'd finished, he pushed back from the table and stood. "What now?"

"Let's go," Brooks said.

Riley followed the two back into the corridor and into the book-filled room that lent a distinguished air to what he knew to be a monster's mansion.

The Master sat behind the broad, gleaming desk. "I presume you're feeling a bit more up to par now?"

Riley nodded. "Good to go."

"Take a seat, Mr. Smith," the man in charge said.

Riley settled into one of four chairs flanking the desk. Brooks stood behind him, Howard maintained his position near the door.

Master reclined in his leather, tufted chair and studied Riley a moment. "You present somewhat of a dilemma, Mr. Smith."

"Look," Riley offered, "I know you have no reason to trust me." He shrugged. "To be truthful, if I had half a chance I'd be out of here in a heartbeat." He held up his hands surrender style. "Whatever's going down between you and Renwick—" he shook his head "—I don't really care. I did this for the money." He locked gazes with the man behind the desk. "But right now, I don't care about the money. Survival will be fine by me. You tell me what I have to do to make that happen, and I'm in."

The Master braced his elbow on the arm of his chair and tapped his chin with his forefinger. "The man you described, Phipps, has been attempting to infiltrate my family for quite some time. That revelation doesn't surprise me in the least. That he finally succeeded is the surprise."

Riley analyzed the concept of *family* the man used. "I can't tell you how he managed the feat." More winging it. "I just contacted the name and number he gave me and I was in."

"I find that quite incredible," Master confessed. "I chose my soldiers very carefully. In twenty years I've never had one betray me."

"His name was Robinson," Riley explained, using the name of one of the men involved with the incident in Alabama. "I called him, and he gave me the job. Considering what happened in Alabama, I'd say you've chosen at least one who wasn't on the up-and-up."

Brooks grabbed Riley by the hair and yanked his head back. "Don't get smart," he hissed through clenched teeth. "Or we'll take you back to the questioning room and bring you down a couple of notches."

"That's enough," the Master scolded his minion.

When Brooks had released him, Riley stretched his stiff neck muscles.

The Master seemed to digest what Riley had said so far. "You were to convince me that I had a mole," Master suggested. "I was expected to accept you into my family where you would gather intelligence about my work and report to Renwick or Phipps."

His *work*. Yeah, right. "That was the plan."

Another of those long, assessing moments passed. "You're very fortunate to still be alive, Mr. Smith. You seem to have made yourself rather invaluable with your announcement."

Anticipation whispered through his veins. Now was the turning point. He was either dead...or in all the way.

"I find myself curious," Master said. "Renwick has his own business. It's low level and quite distasteful. He has neither the intelligence nor the strategic skills to accomplish what I have accomplished."

There was no denying the man's skill at

covering his tracks and running a tight, efficient operation. The idea that he'd gotten away with this unthinkable business for twenty years twisted in Riley's gut. This bastard had to be stopped.

"I suppose Renwick's endgame is to cut supply," Master went on. "When supply dwindles, demand appears to increase, ultimately spiking prices. He cannot hope to offer the caliber of merchandise I alone provide my clients."

The discussion sickened Riley but the more the man talked, the more potential for Riley to learn. "That would be my guess."

Master leaned forward and braced his forearms on his desk. "This turn of events leaves me no choice."

Riley braced for the revelation.

"You're going to sacrifice everything for me, Mr. Smith. Whatever Renwick intended to pay you," he added with a ruthless stare directly into Riley's eyes, "it won't be nearly enough."

Chapter Six

Sitting cross-legged on the floor, Tessa clapped the little girl's hands together as she and the children sang along with the video. The girls giggled and laughed as the song ended.

This was Tessa's favorite time of the morning. The patients had been fed, as had the children. She had an hour of free time with the children. She hugged the little girl in her lap. Sophie had grown so much. Tessa was amazed every day with each new learning adventure. At two years old, the child was already showing indications of being exceedingly bright.

Tessa resisted the urge to smile as she surveyed each of the other three girls. So beautiful. So smart. Milly was five; the twins, Casey and Willa, were four. And sweet little Sophie would soon turn three. She hugged the child again.

No matter what else Tessa did, she had to protect the children. Her arms instinctively tightened around Sophie, who instantly squirmed. But she had to act fast. Time was running out. Fear forced her heart into a faster rhythm. Tessa drew in a deep breath of courage. She couldn't let the fear hold her back.

Their futures depended upon her alone.

Fear could not stop her. She could not fail for any reason.

The door to the children's room opened. Tessa looked up to find Brooks hovering there. Revulsion instantly thickened in her stomach.

"The Master needs you."

"I'm taking care of the children," she said, careful to keep any hint of challenge out of her tone.

"I'll watch the children."

If he'd said he intended to terminate her existence, Tessa wouldn't have experienced a deeper fear. "I—"

"He wants you in the library. *Now!*"

She nodded. There was no arguing. She had been summoned. "Be a good girl," she whispered to Sophie before settling her on the floor.

Tessa pushed to her feet and crossed the room. She hated the way Brooks stared at her when she sidled past him in the doorway. He did things like that when the Master wasn't looking. Leered at her or blocked her path so that she had no choice but to brush close to him when she passed. Even he, however, didn't repulse her as much as Howard did. But both knew better than to touch her or to speak out of turn in any way.

She hurried down the two flights of stairs. The sooner she knew what the Master needed, the sooner she could get back to the children. Brooks keeping watch made her nervous. In no way did she trust the man.

The door to the library stood open, so Tessa walked in without knocking. She drew up short when her gaze settled on Mr. Smith. Howard loitered in the corner.

"Tessa, sit, please." The Master gestured to the chairs in front of his desk.

Surprised to be invited to take a chair, she selected the one farthest away from the man, Smith. He made her nervous in a very unfamiliar way. Desperation had made her give him the information that likely had saved his life until now.

Maybe he had told.

A new kind of fear radiated through her.

If he'd told, she would die. This morning. *Now.*

What would happen to the children, then?

And the patients…

"Tessa, I've explained to you about our guest," the Master offered.

"Yes." He had ordered her to find clothing suitable for the man. The image of Smith's naked body blazed across her mind. She blinked it away. The Master had told her nothing else. But she knew what she'd overheard in the questioning room.

"We're sending Mr. Smith on an errand," the Master explained. "This errand is of the utmost importance to me. I would like you to accompany him to ensure he stays on track."

The bottom dropped out of Tessa's stomach. "Where are we going?" She glanced at Smith, but quickly focused her worry back on the Master. This was the worst thing that could happen. She couldn't leave just now. She needed to be here—with the children!

"Mr. Smith will explain the details once you're on the road," the Master assured her. He shifted his attention to Smith. "I'm confident forty-eight hours will be sufficient time, will it not, Mr. Smith?"

"Since I don't know exactly what you expect of me," Smith challenged, "I can't estimate the required time."

Tessa openly stared at him. Did he not realize that he could not defy the Master in such a way? Tessa gripped the arms of her chair, bracing for the Master's reaction.

The man who ruled her world, as well as that of numerous others, nodded. "True."

Dismay replaced some of the fear. Her gaze swung back to Smith. Who was this man?

"The errand is quite simple," the Master

clarified. "You contact Phipps and ask for a face-to-face meeting with Renwick. My deputies will provide you with the intelligence we would like you to pass along and then you'll return here."

Tessa's heart pounded so hard she struggled to focus on the conversation. This couldn't be happening. It shouldn't involve her participation.

"What makes you think he'll allow me to return?" Smith asked.

"I'm certain you can persuade him with the concept that there is much more to learn now that you're a part of our family."

Smith nodded. "You're setting him up."

"I'm only responding to his actions," the Master countered. "The first move was his. I must protect my family."

Why would he send Tessa away now? "The patients," she said, before she could stop the words. "They'll need me."

"I'll see to their needs," the Master said, a note of censure in his tone. "Forty-eight hours will pass quickly."

Tessa knew better than to question his decisions. "Of course." Her mind spun with thoughts and worries. Her chest ached with…fear.

A rap on the door dragged Tessa's worried gaze from the conversation to the open doorway.

Krant. The technology soldier.

He carried a square box, the size a dozen donuts. The memory of eating donuts with her friends at school flashed. Tessa pushed it away. A distinct fear trickled inside her. She prayed whatever Krant carried wasn't for her.

"I have just the thing," Krant said to his boss, eluding to a prior conversation.

"Excellent." The Master gestured to Smith. "Why don't you brief us all while demonstrating how your technology works?"

Krant moved toward the desk. He sat the box there and removed a circular mechanism. Like a halo or a strange too-small belt made of stainless steel.

"This" he said as he opened the object and reached toward Smith's throat, "locks around the neck like a choker-style necklace. Only it's steel and provides vastly more potential for wow impact."

A click echoed in the room as the necklace locked around Smith's throat. Smith held still but the tension he felt was obvious in his rigid jaw and stiff posture. Was he as in the dark as Tessa? Did he understand what Krant was doing?

Krant turned to the Master. "You have a timeframe in mind?"

Tessa didn't understand any of this.

"Forty-eight hours," the Master said. He considered the clock on his desk. "With a half hour of preparation time to be fair."

Krant made adjustments to the neck band, then dropped his hands to his sides. "Done." He turned to the Master. "Anything else?"

"No. Thank you, Krant. That's all."

Krant nodded, then took his leave.

Tessa clenched her teeth to prevent demanding more information. Demanding would get her sent off to the silent room. A shiver rushed through her at the thought. The silent room was on the top floor next to the Master's quarters. No windows, no light whatsoever…and chains. She shuddered.

"So—" the Master rubbed his palms

together "—we seem to be fully prepared now."

Smith touched the necklace-type device Krant had locked around his throat. "A tracking device?" he inquired.

The Master shook his head. "There's no need for you to wear a tracking device. I feel certain you'll follow my orders precisely."

Tessa felt herself leaning forward in anticipation of what came next.

"Actually the device you're wearing contains a small explosive."

Tessa's gaze locked on the device.

Smith's fingers settled there once more.

"If you do not return here within the forty-eight-hour timeframe the device will activate and..." He shrugged. "There will be quite a disaster for you."

"If," Smith countered, "Renwick detains me?"

"I'm confident you will persuade him otherwise." The Master stood. "Tessa."

Her attention flew to him.

"Prepare for travel. I'm counting on you to keep Mr. Smith motivated."

She pushed to her feet, her legs shaky.

Tessa couldn't find her voice to respond so she nodded before hurrying from the room.

Forty-eight hours. This could interfere with her plans. If anything went wrong… she might not be able to come back. What would happen to the children then? To the patients?

By the time she reached her room, she had calmed herself to a degree. The jeans and sweater she wore were sufficient. She retrieved her overnight bag from the closet and packed the essentials. Toothbrush and paste. A change of clothes. She didn't dare put anything else in the bag for fear of having it found in a search. He would never allow her off the compound without a search.

But then, she couldn't risk leaving anything he might find in her room.

Her fingers rushed over the hangers in her closet until she found the jacket she searched for. She turned the jacket inside out and found the small gap in the lining's hem. She fingered the hole until she fished out the key.

She held the key in her hand; the metal felt like ice in her palm.

Leaving it was out of the question.

Taking it could get her killed.

She had to try.

Moving quickly, she straightened the clothes, including the jacket, in her closet and closed the door. She checked her room to make sure all was neat and orderly. Crossing to the dresser, she studied her reflection. There was only one way that she could think of to get the key out of the compound. She placed the key on the dresser and reached for the hairbrush. Carefully, she arranged her hair into a twist and pinned it securely. Then she tucked the key into the sleek bun. With a hand mirror she ensured that nothing showed.

"Okay." She released a shaky breath. This was the only way. As long as she didn't shake her head too hard, it should stay.

With the ID that identified her as Tessa James tucked into her bag, along with her hairbrush, she left her room. The urge to see the children one last time nearly overwhelmed her, but he would be suspicious of such a move. And he would be waiting downstairs.

Tessa descended the stairs, her shoulders squared, her face clean of emotion.

As she'd suspected, the Master, Howard and Smith waited in the entry hall. Smith had been outfitted with a coat.

"I'm ready," she said in the strongest voice she could muster. This would be the first time she had left the compound without the Master in…ever, she realized. She had never left, unless accompanied by him and his deputies. Her heart stumbled into a frantic rhythm. What did this mean? Why was he sending her with this stranger?

The Master patted her arm. "I'm certain of your loyalty, Tessa. You won't fail me."

"I won't," she promised, the words more breathless than she would have preferred. She wanted desperately to mention the children, the *child* in particular, but he would be displeased if she displayed such uncertainty.

The Master's attention moved to Smith. "I trust you fully understand your mission."

Smith shrugged. "I fully understand what you want, I just don't see it happening.

Renwick is your enemy. I doubt he'll be cooperative."

"You'll find a way," the Master repeated his earlier assessment. "Tessa will keep you on the proper path."

Fear snaked around her spine. "I will," she said to the Master. To Smith she directed, "We will return within forty-eight hours."

He didn't argue with her but his gold eyes failed to underscore that seemingly agreeable silence.

"Howard," the Master said.

Howard stepped forward and handed a small handgun to Tessa.

"To protect yourself," the Master explained with a glance at Smith, "if the need arises."

Tessa picked up the weapon with cold, shaky fingers. "Thank you." She fumbled with the zipper of her bag, then placed the weapon inside.

Howard handed her a cell phone. She placed it in the bag as well.

When her gaze landed on the Master once more, he said, "You know what you have to do. I'll be waiting for your return."

She nodded, unsure what else to say.

Howard opened the door. The blast of cold air sliced through Tessa.

Smith glanced from the Master to her, then walked out the door. She followed, too scared to look back.

Trudging through the ankle-deep snow, she followed Smith to the black SUV parked in front of the house. All other vehicles would be in the massive garage. None were ever left outside unless they were about to be utilized.

Smith climbed behind the steering wheel; she slid into the front passenger seat. She hugged her bag as if it were a lifeline that possessed the ability to save her.

He started the engine, and reality crashed in on Tessa.

Dear God.

This man didn't even know Renwick. She had given him the name. There was no way he could make this happen. No way they could make it back here in time with what the Master requested.

Tears burned her eyes.

She would have no choice.

"Put your seat belt on," Smith told her.

She stared at his profile, her mind unable to fully wrap around the idea that this was actually happening, that she had put herself in this position. Why hadn't she just let the Master and his men do what they would with Smith?

He turned to her. "Seat belt," he echoed.

Releasing her bag, she tugged the belt into place and snapped it securely. Her arms went immediately around her bag once more.

There was plenty she wanted to say, rant mostly, but she couldn't do that. The Master could be listening. The vehicle was likely equipped with a tracking device as well as listening devices. Possibly even a camera.

She had to remain calm. To keep Smith under control…to figure out a way to breach Renwick's security and to do whatever the Master had tasked Smith to accomplish.

Her eyes closed to hold back the tears.

Impossible.

Smith was going to die.

She was going to die.

And the children would have no one to save them.

Fury roared inside her. She forced her

eyes open. No. She turned to the man behind the wheel. He would have to help her.

As far as Tessa knew, Smith was just another horrible man who helped abduct young women and children. Whatever he was or had been in his life, he was about to step into a new role.

One way or another, she needed him to be a hero.

Chapter Seven

The security gates opened and allowed him to pass.

Riley stopped the SUV at the end of the long, winding drive. "Which way to the city?"

Tessa stared at him as if she hadn't understood the words.

"Which way?" he repeated.

Her mouth worked a moment before she said, "Left."

Riley pulled out onto the road, heading left. It had been too dark for him to determine the route they had taken but he had marked the time. About thirty minutes from the bar to the compound.

Until they were out of the vehicle he couldn't risk asking any questions. Their conversation would likely be monitored. The whole damned SUV was probably rigged with tracking and monitoring devices.

He touched the contraption around his neck. It was tight but that didn't bother him. It was the promised charge set to go off in forty-seven hours and fifty minutes. His first task would be to get this thing removed. For that he needed Stark…and a bomb expert. He hoped like hell the New Orleans Bureau office had ready access to that kind of support.

The so-called Master was up to something. It was possible he wanted to test Riley before welcoming him into his family. But Riley had a bad, bad feeling that this whole extreme exercise was about distraction. Something else was going down.

The half hour it took to reach the outskirts of New Orleans felt like a lifetime.

Tessa hadn't uttered a word since telling him to go left. Judging by her posture, she was terrified.

She was another aspect of this situation

he hadn't figured out. Why would she be sent with him?

Riley doubted she represented much of a physical threat. Her alliance to the man who called himself the Master appeared solid.

Except she had given him the information that had ultimately set in motion his survival and escape.

Had to be a setup.

The whole scenario was far too pat.

Riley turned into the parking lot of the first convenience store they reached. He parked directly in front of the entrance and turned to his passenger. "Stay put. I'm going in for coffee."

She blinked but said nothing.

Taking the keys with him, he entered the store. The cashier glanced at him but didn't bother with a greeting. Early twenties, he guessed. A slash of purple brightened her black hair and caked-on dark eye shadow along with the black clothes gave her a goth appearance. He stopped at the counter and hoped like hell she was friendlier than she looked.

"Excuse me. I know this is going to sound like a strange request—"

She laughed. "Man, this is New Orleans, everything is strange."

At least she had a sense of humor. "Do you have a cell phone I could use to make just one phone call?"

Her gaze narrowed. "Why would I let you use my cell phone?"

Riley didn't miss the way she assessed his battered face. "I got into a little trouble last night and I need to call a friend. It's really important."

She pursed her lips and thought about his request a moment. "All right." She pushed the cell phone she'd been tinkering with across the counter. "But if you walk out that door with it I'm calling the cops."

He grabbed up the phone, careful to keep it out of view of the front store windows. "Thanks."

Riley headed to the far side of the store where the coffee maker was stationed. He entered Stark's cell number and checked to ensure Tessa remained in the SUV as he waited through two rings. He needed to be able to see her but he didn't want her to see him using a phone.

"Stark."

"It's Porter," he said, relieved to hear his colleague's voice.

"Where are you? We lost you at—"

"I know," Riley interrupted. "I'll explain everything when we rendezvous. Right now I need you and a bomb tech. One who knows high-tech devices."

"What's going on, Porter?"

"No time." Riley poured a cup of coffee, keeping a close eye on the SUV. "Just tell me where we can meet ASAP. Someplace neutral in case my movements are being tracked."

Stark discussed the possibilities with someone on his end. Ross maybe. Riley couldn't make out the muffled voice, but he knew his Colby Agency colleague was in the New Orleans area and working with Ross.

When Stark came back on the line, he asked for Riley's location. "Hey," he called out to the cashier. She glared at him as if he'd interrupted something important but since there were no more customers in the store that couldn't be the case. "What's the address here?" She rattled it off and he passed it on to Stark.

Stark asked Riley to hold, while he then confirmed the directions he relayed to Riley. "Should take you about fifteen minutes with the lack of traffic this morning."

"See you in fifteen." Riley ended the connection and deleted the number from the cell phone. He returned to the counter and reached toward his back pocket. That was when it hit him that he not only didn't have his wallet, he also had no ID and no money. "Damn."

The cashier rolled her eyes. "Forget it." She held out her hand for her cell.

Riley placed the phone in her palm. "Thanks. I'm really sorry." He hadn't meant to take something he couldn't pay for.

"Don't worry about it." She waved him off. "Just stay out of trouble."

Riley thanked her again as he exited the store. He hoped he could do exactly as she'd suggested.

Tessa didn't look at him as he climbed back behind the wheel. He placed the coffee in the cup holder, realizing then that he hadn't asked her if she wanted anything. He was really off his game this morning.

"You want some of my coffee?"

She shook her head.

Feeling like a total heel, he pulled out of the parking lot and headed in the direction Stark had instructed.

Riley wasn't sure he could tolerate another fifteen minutes of silence in her presence. "Have you met Renwick before?" Seemed like a safe enough question to ask.

"No."

"What's the deal between him and your boss?"

She said nothing.

"I get that they're business competitors," Riley went on despite her refusal to answer. "Seems personal though. More than just competition to own the market." It sickened him considering the market in question.

More silence.

What he really wanted to do was ask her if she remembered who she really was. He wanted to open that line of conversation and just see how deep her alliance to the Master went.

But that couldn't happen until he had some sense of where he stood with her.

She held on to that bag as if she expected a sudden flood and it doubled as a flotation device. Her lack of conversation and the blank expression she maintained prevented him from assessing her state of mind. As they'd left the compound, he'd gotten the impression she was scared, but maybe he'd judged too quickly.

From what he'd seen of the compound, it was an extraordinarily elaborate setup. Howard, Brooks and Krant were the only personnel he'd seen but he felt certain there were others. The large dining table indicated perhaps a dozen on-site.

If there were any captives on the property they, too, had been out of sight. But Tessa would know the answers to all those questions.

Whether or not she would cooperate was the real question in all this.

He had her away from the compound. That was a key element in his operation. But he had no additional details about the organization except the location of the compound. The urge to call in the feds right now, this minute, was overwhelming.

Somehow the so-called Master was counting on the idea that Riley wouldn't take that step. Riley wasn't so sure that the man had bought that fully into his cover. Yet there was something that gave him confidence. By now the compound could have been evacuated and prepared for burning to the ground.

This Master was way too smart and too cunning to let Riley walk out of there with that knowledge. *Unless* he had an ace up his sleeve.

Riley's attention shifted to the silent woman in the passenger seat. She had to be that ace.

The rendezvous location was the parking lot of an abandoned factory in the Ninth Ward. Riley swallowed hard. If they couldn't disarm this thing around his neck, no need to put lives at risk. A deserted location was best for all concerned.

In the daylight, despite the blanket of snow, the ugly scars of the city's worst natural disaster in the last century remained visible. An unmarked van as well as an

SUV waited behind the massive, dilapidated building.

Riley parked the SUV and climbed out. Tessa didn't move. He moved around the hood to her side of the vehicle and opened the door. "Come on," he prompted.

She didn't look at him, kept her attention straight ahead.

"Get out," he said a bit more firmly.

She climbed out of the SUV, the bag still gripped tightly in her arms.

"Leave the bag inside," he said, just in case it was rigged, too.

She stared at him a long, silent moment, then did as he asked.

He shoved the door shut and led the way to where Stark and the others had already emerged from their vehicles. All wore plain clothing, no tell-tale markings of law enforcement.

"Smith," Stark said, keeping Riley's cover intact.

Riley opened his jacket, easing the collar away from the device locked around his neck.

One of the men stepped forward and visually analyzed the device.

No one spoke as the man continued his assessment. He motioned for one of his colleagues to join him. The two used a handheld X-ray-type gadget to see inside the lethal necklace.

When at last they stepped back, the first man spoke. "This appears to be a T.A.T.P.-type explosive. Two chemicals that when combined detonate. It takes a very small quantity to accomplish the goal apparently intended here. The vials can have a built-in time release breakdown component, but in this case there seems to be a tiny secondary charge that will activate via the timer and shatter the vials unless the timer is stopped. Again, this is speculation to some degree since this portable job—" he waved the machine in his hand "—doesn't work as well as the one at the lab."

Sounded bad for him, Riley gathered. "So how do we stop the timer?"

"Can't," the bomb tech said bluntly. "If the timing or the locking mechanism is hampered with the detonating charge will activate. Has to be removed only after it's unlocked, which deactivates the timer. Any unnecessary vibration could set it off."

Tension stiffened Riley's spine. "How do we unlock it?" If that was the only route, then he was ready to get on with it. He understood the additional risk involved with tampering with the lock, but his chances with these techs was likely far better than with the Master.

"It's biometric. We'd need whoever's print it recognizes to get it open." The tech shook his head. "We might be able to override it but that would take serious technology and time."

"If that's what it takes," Stark spoke up, "then we'll take him in. Where's the nearest lab?"

This was bad all the way around. A tug at his jacket drew Riley's attention to Tessa.

"We need to talk." She sent a sideways glance at the other men. "Privately."

Startled that she'd spoken, Riley said to Stark and the tech, "Give us a minute."

The tech shrugged. "It's your head."

No need to remind him of that.

Riley walked a couple of yards away. "What?" As much as he wanted to question her, there was no time for that now. He needed this thing off.

"We don't have time to waste," she said, her expression hard with determination.

"No kidding." Had she missed every word the tech said? "If I don't get this thing off…" She surely understood the ramifications.

She shook her head. "You're not listening."

Riley cleared his head of thoughts of the ticking bomb wrapped around his neck and took a breath. "Explain to me what I'm not listening to."

"If you do not contact Renwick and do as you were instructed, there will be devastating consequences."

No joke. "I got that part." Though he wasn't entirely convinced this was about him or Renwick. But it was still too early to form a reliable conclusion.

She shook her head again, even more adamantly. "I'm not talking about the bomb. Other, devastating consequences."

He searched her eyes. "Are there captives at the compound?" His pulse rate jumped into an even faster gallop.

She nodded. "You don't know what he's

capable of. The children will pay for your failure."

That didn't make sense to Riley. Why would the man destroy the very merchandise with which he dealt? "What would he have to gain by doing that? He has no idea whether I would be swayed by such an act."

"But I would be."

The picture began to clear. "That's why he sent you with me." It was that ace up his sleeve Riley had presumed existed. And she was it.

"If you don't do as he said, the children will die."

He got that part, too. "You know I wasn't sent by Renwick. I don't even know who the hell he is or how to contact him."

She gazed at the men waiting a few feet away, then settled that fierce gaze back on him. "I think I know who you are now. You're a cop or something."

Was that relief he heard in her tone? "Something like that," he confirmed.

"I may know a way to contact Renwick," she said, her voice turning grave. "But we have to move quickly."

"All right. Still, I need to at least go by the lab and see if they can get this thing off." He'd feel a lot more secure without the time constriction.

She shook her head again. "You can go, but I can't do that."

Frustration rose higher, but he tamped it down. "Why can't you do that?"

"He knows where I am at all times."

A new layer of difficulty fell over the operation. "You have a tracking device on you?" He had a feeling it wasn't nearly that simple.

"I have several." She let go a heavy breath. "Implanted. I have no idea the locations. I just know they're there."

Riley knew the rest of the story. If one or more of the devices somehow stopped working or were removed and left at one location, the Master would recognize what they were doing.

Their options were limited to one: follow the order.

He just hoped like hell the man's minions hadn't followed them here and were watching every move they made. That maximized the need to get the heck out of here.

"How fast can you make contact?" There wasn't a single second to spare.

"I'll try now." She looked around again. "But we can't stay here. He knows every inch of this city. We have to keep moving."

Riley stood there feeling defeated for a moment. He couldn't give the location of the compound to the feds for fear someone would screw up and the Master would recognize they were there. He couldn't have the bomb deactivated or removed because there was no time to figure it out.

Once again his survival and that of the mission boiled down to one person.

Tessa.

And even she wasn't sure she could set in motion the chain of events that had to occur to maintain the validity of the operation.

There was one question he had to ask. "Why are you willing to take this risk?" The decision to help him put her at great risk. The motivation to stay involved when the opportunity to walk away was right in front of her had to be immense.

"For the children."

Until she gave him reason not to trust that statement, he had no choice but to go with it.

"Make the call."

Chapter Eight

11:01 a.m.—46 hours,
59 minutes remaining

Tessa waited until Smith had parked the SUV in the cemetery before opening her cell phone.

So far he had gone along with her suggestion to distance himself from his colleagues. She hadn't selected this out-of-the-way derelict cemetery for no reason. The drive from the abandoned warehouse had used up valuable time. But this was her one and only chance to save the children. Her unknowing hero wouldn't be pleased with her plan, but she couldn't let him stand in the way.

Not even if it meant sacrificing his life.

A pang of regret tore through her. It was

hard for her to determine if he was the bad guy she had assumed. She had gotten the impression his friends were law enforcement but she couldn't be certain. He'd said something like that.

If he was a cop, why didn't he just tell her?

If he was an informant, then most likely he had done the same sort of bad things the Master and his soldiers had done. In that case, she had no sympathy for Smith or whoever he was.

Ultimately, her concern had to be for the children and the patients.

Her own life was on the line as well, and she didn't care. All that mattered was saving the children. The idea that she was so far away from Sophie twisted her heart. But it was the only way to save her. Tessa had been planning this operation for a while now. She just hadn't expected it to happen this way...or at this time.

She gently patted the bun of her hair to ensure the key was where she'd tucked it. With that confirmation, she was ready. One phone call—a pretend phone call—and she would make her move. But that pretend call was necessary to keep Smith distracted.

She climbed out of the SUV, the cold air made her shiver. Smith followed her into the center of the cemetery. The slushy snow dragged at her boots.

"This should be fine," she said, acting as if the distance away from the SUV was necessary before making the call.

While she entered the numbers, Smith scanned the woods surrounding the ancient cemetery. He was keenly alert. She would have to stay sharp or he would see through her deception.

"This is Tessa," she said as if the call had connected. She paused long enough to have had a response then said, "I'm ready to work with Renwick. Where can we meet?"

Smith watched her so closely. Fear had her heart pumping hard. Of course he was suspicious. She just needed to ensure he wasn't overly suspicious.

Next she gave her location, then waited again. "Yes, I'll stand by." She looked at Smith then. "No, no, I'm alone." A moment's pause. "Okay." She pretended to end the call and closed the phone. "A contact is on his way here. I told him I was alone—"

"I heard that part."

Definitely ill at ease and highly suspicious.

"Stay down in the SUV," she suggested, "so he doesn't see you right away. Once we determine how many have been sent and how heavily armed they are, we can take it from there. You can use the gun in my bag."

The last seemed to put him more at ease. She followed him to the SUV. As he dug through her bag for the gun he wouldn't find, she snatched up one of the rocks that lined the narrow road that circled the cemetery.

She banged it into the back of his head, tossed the rock and ran.

Afraid to look back to confirm he'd been rendered unconscious, she pushed forward with all her physical strength. The gun in her waistband shook. She put one hand on it to make sure it didn't bounce out.

She hit the woods, underbrush slapped at her legs. Dodging the trees, she refused to slow down even as her lungs burned for more oxygen.

Then she saw it. Her salvation.

Sitting on an abandoned, overgrown old road was the green pickup truck. The vehicle was three decades old but it had run perfectly fine two weeks ago when she, Brooks and Howard had met a contact here.

The meeting had gone sour and the contact had been taken back to the questioning room. As Brooks and Howard had forced him into the SUV, she'd noticed the key to his truck on the ground. She'd picked it up and from that day forward she had planned her escape.

The driver's door opened with a creak. Only then did she dare to look back and see if Smith had followed her. No sign of him. Relief made her knees weak.

She jammed the key into the ignition and twisted it. The starter turned over but the engine didn't roar to life. "Oh, God." She pumped the gas pedal and tried again. The reluctant engine tried to start, sputtering and groaning. "Please, please, start," she murmured.

The engine coughed again then growled to life. She smiled. The movement so unexpected that she reached up and touched her lips. She was going to make it.

She pulled the gear shift into Drive.

Something slammed into the cab next to her door. The truck rocked with the impact.

Her gaze collided with furious gold eyes, and a scream trapped in her throat.

Smith jerked the truck door open.

She stomped the accelerator.

The truck lurched forward.

Smith hung on.

She tried to push him away but he had a death grip on the door and the steering wheel.

Tessa hit the brake hard. The door flopped, sandwiching Smith between it and the cab. He howled a curse.

He elbowed her hard enough to loosen her grip on the steering wheel. His hand reached past her and snagged the key, shutting down the engine.

She fumbled for the gun.

He threw his body atop hers. His hands found the weapon first. She bucked her body in an attempt to throw him off balance.

Too late. He jammed the weapon into her rib cage. "Stop fighting me."

The words were a breathless snarl, but no less threatening.

"Get off me." She shoved at his chest, somehow unafraid that he would actually shoot her. There was something about the way he looked at her that suggested he wouldn't hurt her.

He backed out of the cab, but kept the weapon trained on her. "Get out."

Tessa scrambled out and righted her clothes. Her hair had fallen but she didn't care. Her breath came in jagged spurts. She'd failed. Now her one chance at saving the children…at escaping *him* was over.

After months of planning, she had failed in a matter of minutes.

"What the hell were you doing?" he demanded as he shoved his fingers through his mussed hair.

She ignored him. Rather, she focused on pulling the pins from her hair. One. Two. Ouch. She grimaced. Three. Four. The counting did little to keep her mind off the idea that she was a failure.

She'd let the children down.

She threw down the pins and glared at the man holding the gun. "What do you think I was doing?" She didn't care that her hair was a mess or that he could shoot her any time now. She only cared that she had failed.

"Trying to escape?" he asked, fury making his words as sharp as knives. "Me? Or him?"

"Both," she admitted, not caring what he thought. He had no idea what the Master was capable of. He didn't know anything.

He laughed but there was no humor in the sound. "I thought you were worried about the children. You said you didn't want them to pay for our making a wrong move." He shook his head. "Oh, that was good, lady. The only person you care about is yourself."

She rushed him.

The gun flew out of his hand.

They tumbled to the cold, wet ground.

She kicked at him. Banged her fists at his chest. Cried out with the pain that was ripping her apart inside. He didn't know! He didn't understand!

He rolled her onto her back and pinned her to the ground with his body. His hands were like iron manacles on her arms, holding them down.

"Have you lost your mind?"

She blew the hair out of her face so she could glare at him.

"I could have shot you." He hissed a couple of expletives.

"Shoot me," she dared. "I don't care anymore."

He stared into her eyes, obviously seeing the truth in her statement. The anger in his eyes faded away and sympathy replaced it. That didn't make her feel any better. She didn't need his sympathy. She needed a new plan. *Now!*

Letting go of her arms, he pushed himself upright, then offered his hand to pull her up.

She stared a long moment at his broad hand and the long fingers that seemed to be offering help. But what he offered was just for her…for now. That wouldn't help the children…wouldn't save Sophie.

Despite that cold, hard reality, she put her hand in his and allowed him to pull her to her feet.

"Tell me what's going on with you." His voice was softer now, kinder.

The Master could speak oh so gently and kindly as well. That didn't mean anything. "I knew this truck was here." No point in lying. "I planned to use it to set my plan in motion."

"What plan?"

She looked into his eyes, let him see the hurt and fear in her own. "To save the children. To escape a monster."

He dusted the snow and leaves off his jeans. "How exactly did you plan to do that?"

"I was going to enact the evacuation."

Lines of confusion formed across his brow.

"At the compound," she explained, too weary to fight the inevitable any longer. "We have an evacuation plan if there was the threat of being invaded."

"By the police?"

She shrugged. "By anyone."

He nodded. "I guess he has plenty of enemies."

"More than you can imagine." She closed her eyes and blocked the ugly images. The Master was cruel and uncaring. He had no feelings for who he crossed or who he hurt. Collateral damage was of no concern to him.

"How would the evac plan help save the children?" Smith asked, drawing her attention back to him.

"I know the route." She summoned a deep, calming breath. "He would leave with Brooks." She would be sent with Howard… once he had taken the other steps that terrified her to even consider. "The children and the patients would be Howard's responsibility." Her throat tightened at the idea of what exactly his responsibility was. "I would neutralize him and escape with the children."

"What about the rest of the security personnel?"

"They would act as decoys, unknowing bait, for whoever was invading."

"You assumed you could take Howard on your own," Smith suggested.

She leveled a long, telling look at him. "I know I could take Howard as long as Brooks wasn't around." Tessa considered that point for a moment. The scenario didn't add up. "How did they manage to take you?" She felt confident that at one time the two men had been the best. Otherwise the Master would never have assigned them as his deputies. But they had grown soft and lazy in their higher-level positions, particularly Howard. "You don't seem like the type of guy to be taken by two sloppy thugs."

Smith blinked. To cover whatever flashed in his eyes. She'd caught just a hint of something...challenge maybe. Then she understood. "You wanted to be captured. You let them take you."

He wasn't one of them...he was a cop or something, like he said. She'd sensed that possibility even before the meeting with his colleagues.

Before she could say as much, he said, "Let's just say that things worked out the way I wanted them to."

Dear God. Finally someone had come...

Her gaze fell to the device around his

neck. And in about forty-six hours he would be dead.

"Up to a point," he added, touching the device she stared at.

"We have to contact Renwick," she said. "It's the only way." But there was a problem...that she couldn't tell him about until she was sure she could fully trust him.

His gaze held hers. "What about your plan? Sounds like it could work."

It could. Maybe. But that wouldn't keep him alive.

"We'll contact Renwick. And then we'll go back."

"No—" he shook his head "—I'll go back. You'll set your plan in motion and we'll have backup in place to take care of Howard and Brooks."

"While you die," she reminded him.

"We'll cross that bridge when we come to it." He glanced back toward the cemetery. "Let's do what we have to for now."

He started to turn away. "Smith?"

He turned back to her. "Why are you here? Really?"

"My name is Porter. Riley Porter. I'm here to stop the man you call the Master."

She hurried to catch up with him as he strode through the woods. "Those men back there—" she matched her stride with his "—they're with you?"

"Yes."

"You didn't give them the location of the compound, did you?" If he had…standing orders were to kill the children first. Without Tessa there would be no one to stop that from happening. The Master understood what he would face from the authorities. His motto was to make it worth the sacrifice if the worst-case scenario occurred.

"No, I didn't."

Smith-Porter didn't look at her as he said this. She prayed he wasn't manipulating her. "The children would be killed first, in the event of an unexpected invasion," she told him, hoping he hadn't lied to her. She wouldn't be there to stop Howard. As worthless as he was, he would revel in destroying the innocent lives of those unable to defend themselves.

"There won't be an unexpected invasion," he reiterated.

"I pray you're telling me the truth." This

hadn't turned out the way she'd hoped at all.

As they reached the cemetery once more, he turned back to her. "Trust me, Tessa. I explained that we couldn't divulge that information at this point. The location of the compound remains secret."

The depth of his sincerity had relief washing over her. Still, she found it difficult to believe that the authorities would be this close, because they certainly hadn't ever been this close before, and not want to make a move.

As if he'd sensed her continued trepidation, he stopped again before they reached the SUV. "We're going to bring down his entire network, Tessa." Those gold eyes searched hers. "We're going to rescue the children. That's why I came."

Mixed emotions twisted in her chest. All this time she'd been certain no one was coming. That there wasn't anyone out there big enough or brave enough to be the savior she'd prayed for.

Yet here was this man, standing right in front of her, claiming to be exactly what she'd asked for.

She couldn't help herself. She hugged him. "Thank you." She closed her eyes and inhaled the scent of the man. "I've waited so long for you to come."

His arms went around her, held her tight. "Those aren't the only reasons I came."

She drew back, looked into his eyes. Worry rising again. "I don't understand."

"I came for you."

The air trapped beneath her breast. Was that possible? Could someone out there still care if she were dead or alive?

"One of my colleagues from the Colby Agency," he explained, "Von Cassidy, saw you at the Chicago transfer location. She thought she recognized you." He smoothed a hand over her tousled hair. "You're going to be safe now, Tessa. You have my word."

Chapter Nine

12:05 p.m.—45 hours,
55 minutes remaining

Riley drove to the nearest convenience store. He still had no cash so using a pay phone was out of the question. They'd searched the SUV and the truck for loose change. No such luck. Using her cell phone presented its own kind of risks considering the owner of the account could pull up any and all calls made from the line. Riley had turned off the phone, removed its battery and stored the two in the glove box.

They'd abandoned the SUV in favor of the truck. The tracking devices Tessa believed to be embedded subcutaneously would still allow the Master to monitor their movements, but at least he wouldn't have a description of the vehicle.

The convenience store was a little more crowded than the previous one and the only cashier in sight was male. Didn't bode well for Riley.

"I can do it," Tessa said, looking from the storefront to Riley and apparently understanding his hesitancy.

He wasn't so sure about allowing her to go inside and use the phone alone. As much as he wanted to trust her and felt confident she wanted to bring down this network the same as he did…she was still a risk.

"You don't trust me."

It wasn't a question. His hesitation had given him away. "I want to trust you. But I have to be realistic. You've spent a lot of time with these people. It's only logical that their ideology may have influenced the way you think. Fear is a strong motivator."

She worried her lower lip with her teeth before answering. "I understand."

That was it? He'd expected more.

He made a decision he hoped he wouldn't regret. "You know what, you should do it."

Surprise flared in those pale blue eyes.

"You make the call but there's a list of things we need." He opened the glove box and fished out the pencil he'd noticed there when he'd stored the cell phone. The back of the truck registration would have to work for a notepad.

"This is the number for Levi Stark." He scrawled Stark's cell number. "You met him earlier."

She nodded. "I remember."

"Tell him we need to meet ASAP. Cash, communications and supplies. A scanner to determine if you're carrying tracking devices and portable jammers to use at our discretion. And any word on this." He tapped his steel necklace.

Her eyes widened as if she'd only just recalled the urgency related to the necklace. "Anything else?"

"That's it." He handed her the list.

A frowned formed on her smooth forehead as she reviewed the list. "The jammers are for blocking the tracking devices I'm carrying?" She looked to him for clarification.

"That's right, but we will only use them

if necessary," he assured her. "Be sure to get detailed directions for the meet."

"Okay."

Riley watched her hustle up to the entrance. His fingers clenched around the steering wheel. Forty-five hours. A muscle throbbed in his jaw. He'd been in tight, deadly situations before. But he'd always been able to use strategy to find a way around any obstacle.

There was no logic for this situation. Nothing he could do. He didn't need anyone to tell him that even if he accomplished the goal the Master had set, the man was not going to allow him to live.

Tessa's turn in line came and she smiled broadly at the man behind the counter. Even from this distance the smile was brilliant. He hadn't seen her do that before. Of course, she hadn't actually had that much to smile about in her young life.

He hoped he would be able to help change that.

When Tessa stepped to the far end of the counter, the cashier met her there and appeared to pass a phone to her. Riley surveyed the parking lot and the street behind him. He didn't doubt that one or more of the master's henchmen were tracking their movements from someplace nearby.

He wasn't sure he could do anything about that, since Tessa believed the devices to be embedded. Most likely they would simply have to live with them.

Four minutes passed before Tessa hurried back to the truck. "He'll meet us in half an hour." She thrust a couple of napkins at him. "Detailed directions."

She'd made a lot of notes. Good.

He passed the napkins back to her. "You be the navigator."

Her fingers threaded through her hair as she studied her notes.

Her hair was the most unusual shade of blond. Like the photos of angel hair. Pale, silky, long. Her skin was almost as pale, smooth, soft-looking. And the eyes. The lightest sky-blue. She looked far younger than her age but could talk the talk of the trade when necessary.

He got the impression that to some degree she'd been protected. He hadn't figured out that aspect of her position in the "family" just yet. Maybe when she trusted him more, they could explore those missing years together.

Maybe.

1:15 p.m.—44 hours,
45 minutes remaining

STARK GAVE RILEY THE BAD NEWS.

"That settles it then," Riley announced, hoping to end the debate. There was nothing to be done at this point.

"Mr. Porter," Agent Ross said, his tone grave as he reiterated what Stark had already laid out, "I would strongly recommend that you come with me to the lab and let our specialized techs attempt to take care of this hazardous situation. Before it's too late."

Tessa kept quiet but the widening of her eyes told him she was worried. About him? Maybe. About the kids? Definitely.

Three hours into the countdown and reaching out to Renwick hadn't hit the agenda yet.

Time was running out fast.

"As far as I'm concerned," Riley restated, "the decision is made. We have to go through with the task assigned by this bastard. I believe this is either a test before allowing me into his 'family' or it's a distraction for some purpose we can't see yet. Whichever it is," he said before Stark or Ross could interrupt, "there's only one way to find out."

Stark was shaking his head before Riley finished talking. "I've already spoken to Victoria and Jim. They are not in agreement with that strategy."

Victoria Colby-Camp and her son, Jim Colby, headed the Colby Agency. Going against the chain of command was not the norm at the Colby Agency. But this situation was far too delicate to risk any other route. Victoria, of all people, was well aware of the tenuous situation. An operation involving missing children was different from any other. Jim, her own son, had been abducted as a child. Her granddaughter had been targeted just last year. She might not like what Riley was about to do, but she would understand.

"It's the only way." Riley put up his hands to stop the rest of the protests. "Tessa and I have to get moving. We're all in agreement that time is short. If I hope to survive this operation, much less succeed, we need to work fast."

Ross shook his head. "I can't argue your reasoning, Porter, but there's another issue here."

Tessa moved closer to Riley as if she sensed this was going to be detrimental to the children's safety. Riley could see that coming himself.

"We can't pretend there aren't children at that compound being held hostage," Ross began. "To do so would be wrong on too many levels to name."

Tessa was the one shaking her head this time. "You have to believe me when I say that if the Master so much as feels your presence, the children will die first. You'll have no one to save."

The fear and desperation in her voice tugged at Riley's chest. "She's telling you the truth," he confirmed. His instincts urged him to trust Tessa on that one. Riley preferred following his instincts. "This man is ruthless. He'll do anything to protect himself. If he escapes, he'll just set up shop someplace else in a heartbeat. And what will we have accomplished?"

"I don't doubt what you're saying," Ross agreed. "My point is that we have to do something. Get into position well out of the compound's security zone. I'll use agents and law enforcement from outside the state of Louisiana if necessary. There will be no leaks. We'll stand by until we're told to move in. But, at least, we'll be in position."

Riley looked to Tessa for her reaction.

"I'm certain he has local law enforcement contacts," she said. "If anyone around here knows your plan, he will know it."

"I will personally make sure that doesn't happen," Ross guaranteed.

"And you won't move in until you receive the okay from Riley or from me," she pressed.

Ross balked at that suggestion. "I can't guarantee that stipulation, ma'am. The safety of the hostages must be paramount."

"We're the only ones who will know what's happening in real time," Riley backed her up. "Taking the okay from anyone else would be a mistake."

Ross heaved a frustrated breath. "This could cost me my job, but…agreed."

"And," Riley added for good measure, "I want Stark involved. Up close and personal," he said directly to Ross.

"No problem," the agent allowed. "I'll take anyone from the Colby Agency I can get."

"Jim is calling in markers," Stark passed along, "he's running down the best explosives techs in the country. If anyone can locate someone who can neutralize that contraption, Jim can."

Riley was glad to hear it. Jim Colby wouldn't let him down. If a technique existed, he would find it.

"I don't like the idea that this Master guy will know your every move," Stark said. Ross's team had confirmed that Tessa carried at least three subcutaneous tracking devices.

"If we try to shield the tracking devices he might make a move we're trying to avoid," Riley countered. "We'll only use the jammers if absolutely necessary and for short bursts. We can't afford to make him nervous."

"It's your call." Stark picked up the sports bag at his feet and passed it to Riley. "Cash, ID, secure cell phone, portable jamming device and toothbrushes." Stark smiled but the expression was seriously lackluster. "Anything else?"

Riley slung the bag over his shoulder. "That'll do it for now."

"We've placed a tracking device on the truck," Stark went on, "so we'll know your location at all times. Be warned—" he sent Riley a stern look "—we get down to two hours and we're bringing you in. No matter where you are or what you're doing."

That was likely as close to his way as Riley was going to get. He shook hands with Ross, then with Stark. "Thank you, gentlemen. We'll be in touch."

He turned his back before Ross or Stark could come up with another reason Riley shouldn't go through with this. As far as he could see he had no choice.

Tessa had settled into the passenger seat of the old green truck by the time Riley slid behind the wheel. He placed the sports bag on the floor between them.

Riley started the engine and drove away from the school parking lot. With no school in session, the rear parking lot had worked well as a rendezvous location. He didn't give himself a chance to second-guess his decision about the explosive device. It was the right decision.

"We should make a call to your contact for Renwick." He glanced at Tessa who stared out the passenger-side window. "We've wasted too much time already." Especially considering the decision he'd just made.

She turned to him. "Were you telling the truth when you said you came here to find me?"

"Yes."

Her silence filled the next half a mile or so. "And you're really willing to risk your life—" she glanced at the bomb around his neck "—to save the children and stop the Master?"

They'd been over this already. "Yes." She'd heard the strategy discussion back there the same as he had. Why all the questions now?

She started chewing that full lower lip again. This was a dangerous game she'd been thrust into. He could see how she would be afraid, no matter how strong she tried to appear.

But they couldn't let any more time slip by.

"Make the call," he urged. "We can't wait any longer."

"There's a problem." She stared at her hands as she spoke.

Riley resisted the impulse to scrub a hand over his face. Too many achy bruises for that. "What problem?" They didn't exactly need any more problems at this point. One step forward and two back was getting old.

"I can't make the call."

Riley braked for the stop sign at the intersection, a cold, hard knot of dread forming in his gut. "What precisely does that mean?"

"I know the names." She dared to meet his gaze but only for a second. "I've seen Phipps once. But I don't know him or

Renwick. I don't have their telephone numbers. I don't…know how to reach them."

The dread morphed into something like defeat. She had to be kidding. The whole operation hinged on contacting one of those two.

"I should've told you already," she offered, "but there was never a proper time."

"This is definitely not a proper time." He rolled through the intersection, picking up speed.

He could call Stark. Have him get the names run through the agency's research department. Through the Bureau's system. But those things would take time. They didn't have time.

"I do know," she said quietly, her own defeat evident in her voice, "this one man who might be able to help us. He's done work for Renwick before. I know that for sure. But he might refuse to talk to us."

Hope squashed the defeat that had sprouted in Riley's brain. "You let me worry about that. Direct me to him, and I'll get what we need."

"Okay."

Their gazes met as he braked for the next intersection.

"I won't keep anything from you again."

"That would be helpful." He centered his attention on the road and kept driving as she provided the directions to their next destination.

He wouldn't be cutting her as much slack again. No matter that she'd likely been through things he couldn't even fathom. He needed her on the up-and-up with him. From this second forward.

Those seconds were ticking by way too quickly for his comfort. The steel necklace seemed to tighten at the thought.

"Tell me about this man," Riley prompted, hoping to lessen the tension.

"He's a doctor," she explained. "He takes care of lots of folks who can't afford the regular clinics and hospitals."

"What's his connection to Renwick?"

"He treated him once for cancer."

Riley shot her a look. "What kind of doctor is this guy?"

"He's…different."

Her evasiveness nudged Riley's instincts. "Different how?"

"You'll see. It's difficult to explain. He's just different."

Chapter Ten

2:30 p.m.—43 hours,
30 minutes remaining

The cold invaded Tessa's jacket as she led the way to the home belonging to the man who called himself Moses. The sun had already dropped to the treetops. It would be dark soon. She would be happy to have this part over with before the darkness claimed the day.

The rustic cabin amounted to nothing more than a shack perched on the edge of a swamp. Frigid water lapped at the ramshackle dock, swaying the small boat moored there.

She couldn't recall Moses having any dogs. A shudder rocked through her. She hoped not. Strangely, she was far more fearful of dogs than guns. Maybe because guns had been a part of her life for a very long time…whereas she couldn't remember ever having a dog.

Tessa pushed the thoughts of her past away.

There were plenty of times over the past five years and ten months that she had tried to remember her life before but it was always so painful and dark. The Master told her it was because her parents had abused her, that they had never really loved her. It was best not to try to recall. She had accepted that because it had been easier. Because her very survival had depended upon her acceptance of his ways.

Would she have been able to find the courage to do something to help the children long ago if she'd made different choices? If she had been less accepting?

At the porch Riley moved up beside her and murmured, "Stand to the side of the door just in case. I'll do the knocking."

She nodded her agreement but she didn't think the step was necessary. Moses was strange but harmless. Stories about the old man included many bizarre activities but never violent ones.

When she stood to the right of the door, Riley banged on it with his fist a couple of times.

Tessa listened hard. Music played so softly inside that it was almost inaudible. Did that mean he was home? Wasn't he always home? Rumor was he didn't make house calls. Those who wanted his expertise came to him. She really hoped that was the case.

Riley pounded on the door again.

Tessa moistened her lips and decided not to wait any longer. "Dr. Moses!" She moved closer to the door, ignoring Riley's disapproving look. "Dr. Moses, we need your help."

"Who's we?" echoed through the closed door.

She recognized the voice. A little thin with age but strong and distinct. "It's Tessa, Dr. Moses. We met once before. I'm here with a friend."

Rusty metal squeaked as the door handle turned. Tessa silently repeated the same prayer over and over. *Please let him be able to help.*

He pulled the door open just a crack. She recognized the soft music then, an old Cajun tune she'd heard somewhere. "What kind of help you need?"

Moses stayed out of sight behind the door but Tessa didn't allow that to deter her. "We need to find one of your former patients. It's really important."

The door opened wider then. Moses glared at her, a shotgun held firmly in both hands. "You know the business of all my patients is private." His gaze narrowed as he studied her face. "I know who you are."

Her throat closed a little, making a decent breath impossible. "We've met before." She gestured to the man beside her. "This is my friend, Riley."

Moses eyed Riley skeptically. "He's not from around these parts."

Tessa shook her head. "No. He's from up north."

Moses lifted his chin, calling attention to his scruffy gray beard, as he assessed Riley more thoroughly. "What's that around his neck?"

"Trouble," Tessa admitted. "We need to talk to you about that, too."

Riley sent her a scathing look. She felt confident that he didn't want some swamp-woods doctor taking a look at the explosive device counting down the minutes around his neck.

"Come on in." Moses stepped back. "You're letting Old Man Winter in my house."

Tessa started to step inside but Riley moved ahead of her. She let him. He had the gun after all. Though she wasn't afraid of Moses in the least.

The furnishings and interior were as rustic and eclectic as the exterior and the landscaping. The one unexpected element was the mountains of books stacked all along the walls. More books than even the Master had in his elegant library.

With the aid of a cane, Moses walked over to a table flanked with chairs. Papers were spread over the top so she presumed that was his desk. He propped his shotgun against the wall and gestured to the chairs. "Take a load off."

Tessa joined him at the table. Riley did the same but with a bit more caution. He seemed to still be assessing the place and the man.

"You have a quest?" Moses asked.

Tessa nodded, trying not to show her surprise. One of the stories about Moses involved his ability to see the future. She resisted the impulse to ask him if the children would be rescued safely. The risk that he might say no was far too great for her to bear.

"We need to find a man who can help us accomplish our quest," she explained. "His name is Renwick. I believe you treated him for cancer."

Moses nodded. "I remember the case. The city doctors recommended he get his house in order since his time on this old earth was short. But last I heard his cancer was gone away."

Tessa had heard the same. "Your treatment saved his life." Such as it was. Like the Master, if any man deserved to die it was Renwick.

"I don't like to take credit for such things," Moses allowed, "but that's what they say."

"We need to contact him or his man Phipps," Tessa said, getting right to the point. "You may remember Phipps. Quite tall and thin—"

"Red hair," Moses cut in.

"That's the one," Tessa confirmed. "We need a way to contact one or both. It's very, very important."

"About that?" Moses gestured to Riley's necklace.

Tessa considered keeping that part out of the conversation but she had a feeling Moses would know she was lying. "Yes. And for other reasons."

The old man's dark eyes fixed on hers. "The children?"

Her mouth seemed to fill with grit. "Yes."

"And you?" he ventured.

She nodded.

"You know—" Moses leaned back in his chair "—slavery ended in this country a long time ago. What your Master does is wrong."

Emotion tightened in her chest. "Very wrong."

"Renwick ain't no better," Moses declared, "but he came to me for help. He got a new lease on life and he's repeating the same mistakes. There's a special place in hell for men like him."

The old man got up from the table and crossed the room to rifle through an old chest of drawers.

Tessa dared to make eye contact with Riley then. If skepticism were rain clouds, a dense dark cluster would be hanging over his head.

When Moses returned to the table he tossed a cloth sack in front of Tessa. He pulled out his chair and lowered his frail body there. "There's a bartender at the Rusty Hinge," he said. "Name's Ike. He's one of Phipps's contacts. You convince him to put you in touch with Phipps and you'll be in business."

Hope dared to take root amid Tessa's fears. "Thank you. We really appreciate your help."

Moses untied the strings holding the cloth bag closed, then tossed the contents onto the table. Tessa blinked and looked again to be sure her eyes had not deceived her.

Bones.

She shivered.

Moses looked over the pattern of the bones atop his many papers with great care before lifting his gaze to Tessa's. "The past is catching up with you, child. Your life is about to change in ways you've been afraid to consider." A smile parted his thin lips. "It's all good. No worries." His smile faded. "Unless you trip yourself up with all those bad things that evil man's put in your mind. Be careful, child, you'll be treading a slippery slope."

A new kind of fear trickled into Tessa's veins.

"Now you—" Moses turned to Riley "—your future is a horse of a different color." His attention settled on the steel necklace. "Death is all around you. You might not be able to beat it. That part's not clear in the bones, Mr. Porter. You got a war in front of you. You been lucky your whole life, but luck ain't always enough."

"I appreciate the advice," Riley said, though

his tone sounded more perfunctory than appreciative. He pushed to his feet. "We'll check into the lead you've provided."

"Thank you," Tessa said as she, too, stood. She looked to Riley. "We're glad to support your work."

Riley pulled a few bills from his pocket and offered them to the man. Moses took the money and rubbed it between his fingers.

He nodded. "I'll take it." His gaze moved from Riley to Tessa and back. "This money is clean. That's a good thing."

"Thank you again," Tessa offered. "We don't have much time so we need to be on our way."

Moses held her gaze. "You got less time than you think. Better hurry."

By the time they were in the truck and winding their way along the narrow dirt road worry had worked Tessa's nerves into a frenzy.

"What if he's right?" Parts of what he'd said she hoped were right...but the last. Dear God, time could be shorter than they knew.

"I'm not really a believer in that sort of thing," Riley commented.

If that was supposed to make her feel better, it didn't.

"He's helped a lot of folks," she reminded Riley. "That has to mean something."

"Maybe," he allowed. "There's also a possibility that Renwick's cancer simply went into remission. The same might have happened whether he was treated by Moses or not."

That was true, she supposed. Something Moses had said suddenly poked through the worry. "He called you Mr. Porter."

Riley's gaze bumped hers for a split second. "So."

She shook her head. "I didn't tell him your last name. I only said that you were my friend, Riley."

Riley thought about that statement for a moment. "Maybe you did and you don't remember."

"Do you remember?" she countered.

He shrugged. "Whatever. Which way to the Rusty Hinge? I've been there, but not from here."

She gave him turn-by-turn directions as they went. Her mind wouldn't let go the idea that Moses had warned of a major battle for

Riley. Tessa considered his strong profile. He was a handsome man. Not that much older than her, she thought. Solid square jaw, a little bruised at the moment. Pleasantly shaped nose. His eyes were different. The shade of gold that made her think of sparkling sunshine. Bright and warm and welcoming.

Her attention slid down to the steel band around his neck. What if that thing couldn't be deactivated?

She had dreamed of a hero for so very long. Not once in all that time had she considered that the hero she longed for might have to sacrifice his life to save the children and her.

From the moment she'd laid eyes on Riley in the questioning room, she had sensed something different about him.

Tessa didn't want him to die.

Rusty Hinge, 3:55 p.m.—42 hours, 5 minutes remaining

"THEY'RE NOT OPEN FOR business yet." Tessa scanned the vehicles parked at the side of the run-down warehouse that now served as a hangout for the less than savory members of New Orleans society. She didn't see any that she recognized. Good thing.

If the Master had tried to call the cell phone he'd given her, he, of course, wouldn't get through. But he knew where she was. Ross's people had confirmed that ugly fact.

"We'll wait."

What was wrong with this man? "We don't have the time." She reached for her door. "If Ike's a bartender, chances are he's in there preparing for the night."

"You're not going in there alone." Riley wrapped those long, protective fingers around her arm. "No way."

"No one's going to talk to you about Renwick."

"That may be so, but I can't let you take that risk. At least at the convenience store I could see you." He flung a hand toward the warehouse. "I can't do that here. It's out of the question."

Tessa took a moment, searched his eyes. He did care what happened to her. Not in that overbearing possessive, twisted way that the Master did. But basic human compassion. The kind the master did not possess.

"I'll be fine." She drew in a breath of courage. "I have to do this. We can't waste any more time."

Riley pulled the gun from his coat pocket. "Take this with you."

He was likely to need it more than she, but if it made him feel better…she accepted the weapon and slid its comforting weight into her coat pocket. She reached for the door again.

"Five minutes," he warned. "If you're not back out here in five minutes I'm coming in."

She nodded. Clearly she wasn't going to talk him out of that condition.

Tessa trudged through the muddy parking lot. The day's warmer temperature had melted the snow and turned the ground to mush. The front entrance of the establishment opened with ease, surprising her. She'd expected to have to pound on the door for someone's attention.

A guy mopping the floor stopped and stared at her.

"I'm looking for Ike." She kept her hands in her coat pockets, let her fingers wrap around the butt of the handgun.

The guy jerked his head toward the bar. "He's stocking."

"Thank you." Tessa stiffened her posture and headed that way. Her mind kept ticking off the seconds. Making this happen fast was essential.

"Ike?"

The man behind the bar settled a bottle of whiskey into place before meeting her gaze. He braced both hands on the counter. "If you're here to tell me that you're carrying my child, then get in line. I ain't interested in getting married and I don't make enough here for child support."

His crude comments flushed Tessa's cheeks. "No. Nothing like that." She wasn't quite sure how to respond to his proclamation. "I…I need to get in touch with Renwick. I heard you could help me."

Ike's gaze narrowed. "I don't know who you're talking about."

"Please." She allowed the emotion pressing against her breast bone to show in her eyes. "It's very important."

His expression remained rock hard. "Look—" he glanced around the room "—I don't know who sent you here, but using that name can get you killed."

She nodded. "I know. But I need to reach him. He's the only person who can help me."

Those tell-tale lines of further consideration scrawled across his forehead. "What's your situation?"

"Here's my number." She grabbed a napkin and held out her hand for a pen. Ike pulled the one from behind his ear and tossed it on the bar. She wrote down the number for Riley's secure cell phone. "Tell him Tessa wants to talk to him." She added her name to the napkin to ensure he didn't forget.

Ike picked up the napkin and looked at what she'd written. "I'm not saying I know anyone named Renwick. But, if I did, he'd probably want to know what you want to talk about. Seems to me—" he cocked his head and aimed a condescending stare in her direction "—anybody with a name like Renwick might be a busy man. What's your hook, lady? You can't reel in a big fish without the right size hook and a little appealing bait." He stared at her breasts as he said the last.

Fear rattled Tessa's bones but she refused to let this ape see it. "Tell him I need a long vacation. I'm ready to make a move that would benefit the both of us."

"All right." Ike shoved the napkin into his shirt pocket.

She needed him to make the call now! "There's a time limit."

His eyebrows raised in surprise. "You got a short shelf life, baby? You going bad or something?"

A tremble rippled through her despite her best efforts to contain the reaction. She was stronger than this. "What I am," she said sternly, "is a woman with a valuable commodity. If I don't hear from him within the hour, I'll move on to someone with more to offer."

"Funny," he said, calling her bluff, "you seemed a little desperate just a minute ago."

"I got your attention, didn't I?"

He laughed. "Yeah, you sure did."

"Then you'll call him now," she pressed.

He straightened away from the bar and heaved an impatient breath. "Sure." He motioned to the boxes of whiskey and liquor. "You can see I don't have anything else to do."

"Thank you." Tessa's knees almost buckled as he walked to the other end of the bar. She glanced back at the entrance. Riley hadn't come busting in yet.

The bartender made a call on the bar's phone, seemed to be speaking to someone. He looked back at Tessa, then turned his back.

Her heart rate climbed a little faster. Her fingers felt numb.

She checked the entrance again. Still no Riley. She doubted that would be the case much longer.

Finally Ike the bartender ambled back up to where she waited. He passed her the napkin she'd written on. "He'll call you."

"Soon?" That the one word came out so hopeful and desperate frustrated her.

Ike shrugged. "I can't say, but I can tell you that he sounded interested in your proposition."

"Thank you."

When she turned away, the bartender stopped her with a "Hey." Tessa looked back to see what he wanted.

"Renwick's a bad dude. You better consider all your options before you go that route."

She nodded. "Thank you."

He shrugged. "Just saying."

Walking as quickly as she could without breaking into a run, she made the door and was out of the building just in time to come face-to-face with Riley.

"Renwick's going to call. He wants to talk," she said, unable to catch the breath that had suddenly disappeared from her lungs. She chose not to tell him all that she'd said. He would insist that she'd put herself at far too much risk.

The cell phone rang, preventing Riley from asking any other questions.

He handed the phone to Tessa, his gaze heavy on hers. He was suspicious. She could see it in his eyes, could feel it emanating from her posture. Somehow she'd given herself away. She wasn't very good at hiding her feelings. Immense discipline had been required to hide her true feelings from the Master. She hadn't had time to develop that discipline with Riley.

But there was no time for him to question her now.

The cell rang again.

She opened it. "Hello."

The sound of the caller's voice sent a chill straight to her bones.

It was *him*.

Chapter Eleven

It was dark.

Matched his mood.

Riley could not believe what Tessa had done. What the hell had she been thinking? This meeting was supposed to be about what Riley had to offer—not her!

Since having a scene in the parking lot of the Rusty Hinge wasn't a smart move, they'd driven to a more anonymous location. On the northern outskirts of the city, a truck stop had worked. The parking lot was huge and the big trucks provided plenty of cover. Yet the good lighting prevented anyone else from loitering nearby to keep an eye on them.

"I will not let you put yourself in that position. End of negotiations, Tessa."

She glared at him, her lips compressed with fury.

"I know you want to save those children." He did. And he understood that. "But you're a victim, too. I won't trade one victim's safety for another. We have to find a different approach. Make it about what I have to offer."

"Four children are in that compound, Riley," she threw back at him. "Four. There are four young women—younger than me—who are due to deliver any day. That's a total of twelve lives." She planted her hands on her hips. "You're not thinking logically. You are an unknown variable. Renwick knows I'm deep in this organization. He will be more likely to take that bait."

She was out of her mind. *She was*. "I see your reasoning," he agreed. "I do. But what you're trying to do is my job. That's why I'm here, to save you and the others. If anyone is going to take this kind of risk, it's *me*."

Her hands went up in exasperation. "So

it's okay to sacrifice you, but not me." She shook her head. "Sorry, but I don't see it that way. You're innocent of any crimes here. I've been a part of this organization for almost six years." She blinked back the emotion shining in her eyes. "I've been a part of things...that I can't even bring myself to talk about." She stuck her thumb in her chest. "This is the least I can do to absolve myself."

"No way." He shook his head. "I don't care what you think you're guilty of, there were extenuating circumstances. You are not one of them!"

She stared at him with those pale blue eyes. "Yes. I am. I've known dates and places and—" she shook her head "—everything. I didn't try hard enough to stop him. I have this chance and I'm not going to fail."

He looked away. Couldn't bear to see the anguish in her eyes. Nothing he said seemed to be getting through. They had argued all the way here and for another twenty minutes since.

Riley cleared his head. He needed to think rationally. He was allowing far too much emotion to intrude on this case. Maybe because he had a younger sister about Tessa's age. He couldn't imagine having her go through what Tessa had likely gone through. Not to mention his parents. An unimaginable nightmare.

After a time to get his head on straight, he said, "Let's look at this practically. We have something Renwick wants, obviously."

"I have information he will want," she offered.

Riley gritted his teeth a second to hold back the anger and frustration. "And we have the mock operations intelligence that Master provided." Riley would wager that Renwick would want more than anything to bring down this so-called master. "Competition in the marketplace" as the Master had so aptly pointed out.

Renwick or his contact, most likely a contact, would meet with Tessa at 8:00 a.m. That was the earliest time he would agree to. Didn't leave as much time as Riley had hoped for to wrap things up but it would have to do.

They could hedge their bets by Tessa holding out on certain information until

Renwick made a move against Master. She'd set up that strategy already without realizing the benefit of the tactic.

Maybe, just maybe, this could work.

"But what if he refuses to act on the information?" Tessa asked, her voice too quiet. She was exhausted and suddenly second-guessing herself.

"Then we'll refuse," he said simply. He started the truck's engine. "We need a place to crash. Sleep will make this all look better in the morning." Riley wasn't so sure how much sleep he would be able to get, but Tessa needed rest.

"But…" She touched her throat. "What about that? By the time we meet with Renwick or his contact we'll be almost to the halfway mark in how much time we have."

"Don't worry." He shifted into Reverse and backed out of the parking spot. "Once the first domino falls it'll all go down in a hurry."

Riley drove until he found a low-end motel called The Oleander well off the main thoroughfares of the city. Something close enough for quick action, but well out of the way of the mainstream. Before checking in, he picked up sandwich fixings and drinks at a convenience store. Food was necessary for optimal clarity and awareness.

He got the room and paid in cash. Thankfully the rooms were small, stand-alone cottages. No shared walls. The place smelled of disuse and neglect, but it would have to do.

While Tessa showered he set up a monitoring device just outside the door. Since it was the only entrance, chances were if someone showed up that would be the way they would attempt to get inside. He didn't want any unexpected guests.

Once the door and one window were secured, he closed the drapes. He placed a call to Stark and passed along their position. Two agents would be checking into a hotel closer to the city but only a few miles from The Oleander in case they needed backup.

The agency's attempts as well as those of the Bureau to ID the man who deemed himself the Master had proven futile. While Ross's explosives tech had assessed the device wrapped around Riley's neck, another of his people had lifted prints from the cell phone the Master had given Tessa. Nothing popped up except a confirmation that the woman with Riley was indeed Tessa Woods.

He'd known that was the case. Her parents had been notified. Whatever happened to him, Riley had to keep her alive—for her family's sake. He didn't want to be the one responsible for them losing her a second time.

The bathroom door opened and Tessa emerged wearing the same clothes as before. Her hair was still damp. Riley couldn't stop the smile that tugged at his lips. She didn't appear to care about makeup or the latest in hairstyles. Jeans and a simple blouse appeared to suit her without the fuss of designer names or high fashion. Tessa Woods, despite the horrors that had befallen her, had grown up to be a beautiful, compassionate woman.

That totally blew him away.

She'd had every reason not to.

"I hope I left you some hot water." She scrubbed at her damp hair with the towel. "It felt really good."

He thought about the first time he'd seen her in the pink flannel gown that covered her body from her neck to the ankles. Even then she'd looked soft and sweet and alluring. Right now, she looked sexy as hell.

"Riley?"

He snapped out of the daze just looking at her had drawn him into. "I'll shower later."

She hung the towel around her neck and wandered to the small table by the window where he'd spread out the meal options. Peanut butter, ham spread, cheese and bread. Chips along with bottled water and sodas should keep them fueled.

"Want a sandwich?" she asked.

"Definitely." He joined her at the table. Standing close to her, he could smell the shampoo she'd used. Honey scented. He resisted the urge to lean toward her.

She opted for peanut butter and a soda. He slathered on the ham spread and a couple of slices of cheese. With the bag of chips under one arm and his drink and sandwich in hand, he plopped down on one side of the bed. She walked around the room a couple of times. He pretended not to notice her uneasiness. Finally, she perched on the other side of the bed.

They ate in silence for a time. He liked watching her nibble at her food. Slow, methodical little bites. He wondered if she'd been trained to eat so slowly and carefully.

She caught him looking at her. Again.

"You a vegetarian or you just don't like ham?" he asked, mostly as a distraction from the route his mind appeared determined to take.

"One of the children has a peanut allergy so we're not allowed to have it. Ever."

"That's too bad."

"It's scary."

"You said there were women there due any day," Riley ventured. He didn't want to push her for anything she didn't want to talk about. That was a shrink's job. But he wanted to know her better. He'd test the waters and see where the conversation went.

Tessa sipped her soda, then set it on the bedside table. "They're pregnant. The hope is that the babies will have the right coloring. Blond hair and blue eyes are the most valuable." She said this without looking at him as if the topic humiliated her. "They're not always easy to find."

Damn. Riley couldn't fathom that kind of inhumane rationale. "Is that why he chose you?" he dared to ask.

She nodded. "There have been others." A small shrug lifted her shoulders and let them fall. "There will be more if he isn't stopped."

He let the conversation go while they finished their sandwiches. There were a hundred questions he wanted to ask. The children they'd recovered in Alabama had all been abducted. Had he sought out young blond-haired, blue-eyed pregnant girls, too? Or worse, had he arranged their pregnancies after he abducted them?

Was that how the four children currently at the compound had come to be there? Why the women were due to deliver any day? Why keep those four and not ones from the Alabama operation unless that were the case? How was the selection of women made? What criteria were used besides hair and eye color?

"He receives requests," Tessa said

eventually. "Sometimes for Asian children, sometimes African American. Most of the time the clients want children six years of age or older, but no older than eighteen. And there is always, always a high demand for Caucasian female children with blond hair and blue eyes."

"You said they're not always easy to find. How does he handle that problem?" That was the closest way he could think to ask the question burning in his brain.

Tessa got up and discarded her soda can and napkin. She took her towel back to the bathroom and then moved about the room as if she were looking for something. He didn't rush her or prod for an answer.

When she'd decided to sit again, she met his gaze with a somber one. "Ten years ago he started producing and harvesting what he couldn't so easily get his hands on any other ways."

The horror he'd seen in her eyes several times since they met now formed a massive weight on his chest. "The young pregnant women?"

"Yes."

"How…" Again he felt uncertain of how

to broach the question. "How can he be sure of the desired coloring?"

"He selects the surrogates—the young women."

Riley struggled to keep the disgust from his face.

"Then, using an insemination process, they are impregnated with carefully purchased donor sperm meeting all the necessary criteria." Her voice sounded dull, listless. "It's all very clinical. The women are monitored closely. Given proper medical care and the best nutrition possible."

"What happens to the women when the babies are born?" This was like something from a horror film.

"They're given three months rest and the process starts again." She looked away, exhaled a halting breath. "Until they're no longer useful."

His own chest felt too heavy to allow his lungs to fill with air. "What about the babies? Even with parents who have the right coloring, brown eyes or brown hair, or whatever, can show up."

"Happens sometimes." She picked at the crumbs she'd dropped on the bedspread.

"Those babies are less valuable but represent a marketable commodity just the same. Buyers are never a problem."

He wouldn't ask the other question throbbing in his brain. As badly as he wanted to know her role in the organization, he would not ask. Like the rest, she would tell him in her own time.

"Where do you live?" she asked, her voice small as if she feared it was a question she might not be allowed to ask.

"Chicago now." He gathered his trash and disposed of it. "But I grew up in Kansas City. My parents still live there. My sister's in college there. She's going to be a teacher."

One of those rare smiles pulled across her lips. "I'd like to be a teacher." Shame abruptly clouded her face. "I could never be a teacher now...not after what I've done."

Riley reached across the bed and took her hand. "What happened to you wasn't your fault." She lifted her gaze to his. "You're a victim. When this is over, you'll have the opportunity to start your life over and be anything you want to be."

She drew her hand away as if she feared

the connection would reveal something she wasn't ready to confess. "Do you see your family often?"

"Couple times a year plus I usually try to make the big holidays."

"You don't have a wife?"

"Not yet. Maybe one day."

"Girlfriend?"

He laughed. "Not lately."

"I haven't had a boyfriend since I was seventeen." She managed a small laugh. "I'm a high school dropout with a lengthy résumé of criminal activities." She shook her head.

"You are not a criminal, Tessa," he repeated softly. "You're a victim who has done what she had to in order to survive. Don't forget that."

"So many times," she murmured, "I've wished so hard just to be normal. To be like any other woman my age."

"It's never too late," he offered. "As long as a person's breathing there are opportunities and possibilities."

Riley wished he could take that distant sadness from her eyes, but he didn't have that power. Only Tessa could decide to set a course that would make her happy. To achieve her dreams.

But what he could do was protect her.

She tugged at a lock of her hair, twisted it around her finger. "You said you go home for Christmas?"

"Usually, but not this year."

She opened her mouth, then closed it. "Oh. You missed it to do this."

"This is important. My family understands."

"Your family has a big tree and all the trimmings?" Something sparkled in her eyes, maybe a distant memory from her life before.

"My folks go all out." He smiled. "Christmas and Easter are really big deals at the Porter homestead. My parents are desperate for grandkids."

"I always see the Christmas trees in town." Her gaze took on a far away look. "They made me think…"

She didn't finish the thought but he had an idea what she'd intended to say. "You don't want to talk about your family?" he asked carefully.

That blank expression she'd been wearing

when he first met her claimed her face. "I don't have a family anymore." She shook her head. "Not that family anyway."

Riley wasn't sure how much he should tell her, but he couldn't let her spend another moment feeling this way. "I did some checking before I came to New Orleans."

She fiddled with the hem of her blouse. "I guess that's part of your job."

"Yeah. I looked into how your folks are doing."

Tessa practically jumped to her feet. "I should brush my teeth."

Should he push the subject?

"They're doing as well as can be expected under the circumstances."

She searched through the sports bag Stark had provided.

"Your father retired. He's writing a book."

"Here we go." She drew a toothbrush out of the bag, then the toothpaste.

"Your mother started a support group for broken families. She's quite a powerful speaker and highly sought after."

Tessa moved to the sink, which was outside the actual bathroom cubicle.

"Your brother graduates from law school next year. He's engaged to the same woman he's dated since high school."

"Karin." Her voice was small, almost too soft to hear.

Riley waited for Tessa to say more.

"Her name is Karin." Tessa stood before the sink, staring at him via the mirror, the loaded toothbrush in her hand.

"That's right," he confirmed. "She graduated from college last year. She's a nurse now."

"Nurse." Tessa wasn't looking at Riley anymore, she was looking back into her past. "She always wanted to be a nurse."

"She was your best friend all through school," he reminded Tessa.

"She used to play nurse with our dolls." Tessa set the toothbrush down.

"They all miss you," he dared.

She turned to face him. "They can't love me now." She shook her head. "Not after what I've done. They won't understand." Tears streamed down her cheeks.

Riley stood and crossed the room to ensure she saw the truth in his eyes. "They will understand. And they'll always love you." He swiped the tears from her cheeks with his fingers. "None of this is your fault."

She peered up at Riley. "There are things I can never tell anyone," she whispered.

"I know." He watched as another tear rolled down her cheek. He brushed it away with the back of his hand. "You don't have to share anything you don't want to until you're ready."

"I'm scared." She shook her head. "You can't imagine how scared."

As if to underscore her words she trembled. Riley pulled her into his arms and held her close. Her heart raced against his chest. He gently smoothed her hair. Kissed the top of her head. The tears turned to sobs. She shook against him.

He murmured all the soothing words in his vocabulary. Nothing he could say would likely be exactly what she needed to hear, but he had to try.

And maybe what she needed more than anything else right now was to feel the touch of someone who wanted to protect.

Someone who intended to save her no matter the risk.

Chapter Twelve

Monday, December 28, 5:20 a.m.—
28 hours, 40 minutes remaining

Tessa's eyes opened. The room was dark save for a dim shaft of light. Terror wired her muscles for several seconds until she regained her bearings. Motel. She turned her head to the right. Riley lay beside her. She'd awakened several times during the night, and he'd always been awake. He likely hadn't gotten much sleep.

Too busy watching over her.

Protecting her.

She turned that thought over in her mind. The Master had protected her. Ensured she had food and water, clothing, medical care. But his protection was different. He didn't simply protect her…he controlled her. Used her. She shuddered inwardly. How had she allowed him to do that to her for so long?

She should have stopped him.

Memories and worries whirled so fast in her head that she felt sick to her stomach.

Tessa closed her eyes and silently recited the facts.

The Master would have killed her on the spot had she defied him.

She had resisted in the beginning. God, she'd been so scared. He'd locked her in one of the cells in the questioning room. He'd forced her to watch him torture those who crossed him. Days had passed with no food and scarcely any water. Over and over again he and his deputies had taunted her.

Your family doesn't love you.

They aren't even looking for you.

They're glad you're gone.

Days before her abduction she'd had a huge fight with her parents. She'd screamed ugly words at them.

I hate you!

I can't wait to be away from you!

You love Jason more than you love me!

Her brother Jason hadn't even been at

home. He'd been away at college. Still she'd been envious of the way her parents had boasted about his academic and sports accomplishments. Full scholarship. Most valuable player. The perfect son.

Tessa had only been angry. She hadn't meant any of it.

Still, her own final words to her parents had lent credence to what the Master told her. He'd twisted her confessions to make her believe her family hated her and didn't care if she ever came back. Their son was all they needed.

Finally, physically and mentally exhausted, she'd broken. She'd clung to what he offered, had accepted him and his people as her new family.

Deep inside she'd known it wasn't real. Make believe. All pretend.

Her life was like a theater production. She played the part and as long as she was good she could count on the status quo.

That was all she'd hoped for. Another change would have broken her mind completely.

Then Sophie had been born.

Tears welled in Tessa's eyes. In the past

three years everything had changed for her. She'd grown strong again. Her position as caretaker for the children and the patients had fueled her courage. She was all that stood between them and the others—men like Brooks and Howard. Every challenge, every triumph had made her stronger.

Then she'd started to plan a way to escape.

She turned her face back to Riley's. The faint line of light from the bathroom highlighted his features. Even bruised and battered he was beautiful. God had sent her a savior. She'd prayed for so long. Tessa had begun to think that God had forgotten about her or that she had been too evil for His attention.

Her gaze moved over the steel band around Riley's throat. Her chest tightened with renewed fear. What if the Master refused to remove it?

He should have put it on her. She was the one who deserved to be in that position.

Riley's eyes opened.

Her heart stumbled. "Morning."

He smiled. Her heart stumbled a second time. No man had ever looked at her that way and smiled. She barely remembered dating in high school. Not that she'd had that many dates and even fewer kisses.

"Morning," he mumbled.

"You didn't sleep much," she acknowledged.

"Enough," he countered.

"Are you afraid?" She touched the steel band. Shivered at the stark, cold feel of it.

"No. Mostly I'm ticked off about it." He reached over and smoothed the hair from her cheek with the tips of his fingers. "Stark or Ross will think of something."

The man had no guarantee of surviving beyond the next twenty-eight hours and he was as calm as could be. And the manner of death looming over him was far, far from any semblance of a decent way to die—if such a thing existed.

"Are you afraid?" he asked.

"Yes." Despite what was ahead of them she liked lying here next to him. It felt *normal*. Something she hadn't experienced for a very long time. The feeling prompted her to be totally honest.

"You're worried about the meeting?"

She thought about that for a moment. "Not so much."

"The children?"

"Yes. For sure."

"We'll do everything in our power to protect the children and the women," he promised. "If there is any way on earth to rescue them unharmed, Stark will ensure it happens."

Tessa blocked images of Sophie from her mind. She couldn't go there. Not and face what lay before her. Right now objectivity was extremely important. That was one part she couldn't be fully honest about just yet. But soon. She wanted to share that one happiness with Riley.

"You hungry?"

Strangely, she was. "Yes."

"Let's see what we can do about that." He raised up onto his elbow. "There's gotta be something close by that serves a hot breakfast."

"Pancakes?" She loved pancakes. The Master only allowed them on special occasions.

Riley laughed as he sat up. "Pancakes it'll be then."

5:50 a.m.

RILEY DROPPED THE KEYS in the manager's box mounted on the office door. He surveyed the area as best he could considering it was still dark. No traffic on the road. No parked vehicles anywhere within view of the few streetlights. But there was a lot of dark space, a lot of shadows too close for comfort. Someone could be out there, watching and waiting.

Tessa waited in the truck. He walked around to the driver's side and climbed in. "Keep an eye on your side mirror as we head back into town." Staying on top of the situation as much as possible would increase their chances of success.

"You think they're watching us?"

He backed up and pulled out onto the road. "Don't know for sure, but I'm guessing they're keeping tabs on us. The Master's too smart to let us run loose like this. We know too much." Like the location of his compound. Just didn't add up in Riley's estimation. This entire operation didn't sit right with him.

The cell phone rang. Riley reached

into his pocket and checked the caller ID. Blocked number. Most likely Renwick or one of his cronies. "I guess you'd better answer this." He passed the phone to Tessa. Making their contact skittish would only steal more of their limited time.

"Hello."

Tessa listened for a long enough span of time to make Riley nervous. "We'll be there," she assured the caller finally. She stared at the phone a moment before closing it and passing it back to Riley.

"Renwick?"

"No. It was Phipps. He's meeting us at seven-fifteen at New Orleans Park."

"That's what? A public park?" Now that really surprised Riley. Nothing about this operation was the expected.

"Very public." She looked behind them but Riley had kept an eye on the rearview mirror while she was on the phone. "Even at this hour and this time of year, that area isn't going to be completely deserted."

"Did his tone give you any reason to suspect something was up?" Riley was good at assessing voices and body language. Tessa might or might not be so skilled.

"No." She relaxed into her seat. "He sounded calm and cool. Ready to get down to business."

Just another fact that stacked the unexpected deck.

"Why don't you check your cell phone and see if you've missed any calls?" If he'd known Tessa was loaded with tracking devices he wouldn't have bothered shutting down that phone. The Master had known their every move anyway. But hindsight was twenty-twenty.

Tessa placed the battery back in the phone and turned it on. Thirty or so seconds later she said, "No missed calls. No text messages."

If the bastard had been watching them he either didn't care that they'd met with law enforcement officials or he'd known that was coming.

The idea made Riley all the more uneasy. His instincts were screaming at him that this whole operation was way, way wrong.

"I have an addition to the plan." Tessa turned to him. "I think it might actually work better."

A change at this stage in the game could be dicey. Particularly when Riley hadn't been made privy to it before now. "When did you make this decision?"

"This morning while I watched you sleep."

He met her gaze. What he saw there had him experiencing a tightening deep in his belly.

"I need this to work."

He nodded. "Okay. Let's hear the details."

"I'm going to lead Phipps to believe that I want part of what I'm offering. Makes the whole story more credible if there's something in it for me."

As Tessa explained, Riley's ability to breathe became more and more difficult.

She was right. This could work.

For both of them.

The scary part was that her plan was logical and nothing so far related to the Master had come even close to logical. Maybe that was how he'd stayed in business this long...everything about with an unexpected twist.

7:00 a.m.

IT WAS A LITTLE WARMER this morning,
but Riley kept his coat zipped to his throat
to hide the steel band from view. He didn't
need Renwick's people getting any ideas
about his situation. Or the level of desperation involved in this transaction.

Tessa had wanted to meet Phipps alone
but Riley had drawn a line and refused
to budge. He had allowed her to take far
too many risks already. The weapon was
tucked into his waistband beneath the coat.
He was as ready as he was going to be.
Stark and Ross had no choice but to stay
way back. Any sign of cops or trouble and
the meeting would be off.

Scattered pedestrian traffic, as Tessa had
predicted. Park employees mostly. Riley
was antsy. He had infused his veins with
caffeine at the pancake house. A smile
tugged at the corners of his mouth when
he considered how Tessa had dug into the
mound of blueberry pancakes. She hadn't
been exaggerating when she said she loved
them. He wouldn't have expected someone
so thin to have such an appetite.

She'd told him this morning that she was scared. He wondered if so much freedom scared her a little, too. Almost six years had passed since she'd walked around anywhere of her own free will.

He'd had buddies in the military who'd spent time as prisoners within the enemy camp. The horror stories of never knowing when you would be allowed so much as the choice of which beverage you preferred still held a prominent position in their memories. Of course, that had been the least of their worries.

He couldn't imagine how many nights Tessa had lain in bed wondering if she would die the next day or be abused in some nightmarish way.

She'd gone through too much already. He wanted her away from these people ASAP.

"That's him," she murmured with a glance toward the west end of the park.

"I see him." A cap hid the red hair Riley had been watching for. The heavy coat made him look a little heavier than Riley had anticipated from Tessa's description.

Phipps strolled casually in their direction.

No hurry, no visual panning of the area. The man didn't appear to be at all concerned about a setup.

Just another aspect that bugged Riley. Why hadn't the Master enacted his evac plan as soon as Riley showed up with the news that he might have a mole in his organization? Was he so confident in his local law enforcement contacts that he didn't worry?

It seemed Renwick's people operated the same way. Far too much of a coincidence to sit well with Riley. But just because Phipps had entered the park alone didn't mean backup wasn't nearby. In Riley's experience a guy didn't reach the level Phipps had without reasonably good strategy skills. And sharp instincts.

Tessa stood very still without saying a word as the man came closer.

He stopped just beyond arm's length and looked from Riley to Tessa. "Who's this?"

"You know the Master doesn't allow me to go anywhere alone." Her voice was steady and strong despite the extreme fear he knew she felt.

"I thought you were done with the *Master*." Phipps sneered with another suspicious glance at Riley.

"I'm ready to move on to bigger and better things," she agreed. "We're both finished with him."

Phipps snickered. "So you got yourself a sidekick, did you?"

"A personal bodyguard," Riley corrected. He lifted his jacket just enough for Phipps to see the weapon in his waistband.

"What does *he* have to say about that?" Phipps asked, his expression and his tone oozing derision. "Renwick says your nickname is 'His.'"

Tessa held her ground. "Things have changed. Do you want to hear my proposal or not?"

Phipps shrugged. "Impress me, and maybe I'll take your offer to Renwick. Otherwise I'm not wasting the man's time."

Riley kept an eye out for trouble, but this close there was no way to miss the man's hate-filled nuances. He seriously had an ego problem.

"I have the pertinent data for the next four transfers," Tessa told him. "All involve a dozen or more girls. He has a meeting today with a new buyer. I can give you the details of the meeting. In addition, I'm willing to provide you with the account number for one of his primary overseas accounts. This offer has two conditions."

She had his attention now. Phipps's expression shifted to one of keen interest. "What conditions?"

"First, I want out completely," she said. "I have no interest in belonging to you or to Renwick."

Phipps looked her up and down. "Too bad for me."

A burst of fury roared in Riley's gut. He had no right to feel anything even remotely related to jealously but he couldn't suppress the reaction.

"Second," Tessa went on, "I want half the money from the account to start a new life."

Phipps laughed long and loud. "You can't be serious."

Riley hooked his thumb in his front jeans pocket.

Phipps noticed. "How much money are we talking about?"

"There's four million in the account," Tessa told him. His eyes widened. "You get two and I get two." Before Phipps could argue, she added, "There'll be a lot more than two million in it for you when you take over his territory. All you have to do is terminate him and its all yours for the taking."

The man's gaze narrowed with skepticism. "I'm having a little trouble wrapping my head around your proposal. How would you have access to his money accounts?"

"The Master's getting older. He's not as sharp as he used to be," she said bluntly. "He's come to trust me far more than he should have."

"Obviously," Phipps quipped.

"Whether you wrap your head around the concept or not," she pressed, "this is what I have to offer. If you're not interested I'm sure one of his European competitors will be."

Again, she had the man's attention.

Riley decided that Tessa's brother wasn't the only one who had adjudication skills. She would make a damned good lawyer. But then, she'd said she wanted to be a teacher. The part that made him feel good was the idea that she would get to make the choice.

"I'll need to present this to Renwick." Phipps adjusted his coat. "How much time do I have?"

Tessa looked him square in the eye and said, "Five minutes." Indignation captured his expression. "Starting four minutes ago," she added.

Riley was duly impressed.

Phipps, not so much so. He reached into his coat pocket. Riley's hand moved under his coat.

Phipps showed his cell phone. "Chill. I have to make a call."

He stepped a few feet away and made the call. Tessa exchanged a look with Riley that revealed the sheer terror throttling through her.

He gave her a nod. She'd done a stellar job. Truth was, he doubted he could have done any better himself. Her negotiation instincts were right on the money and she'd stood her ground as good as any man.

Phipps returned to their huddle. "Renwick says it's a go. First we'll divert the account balance and then we'll set up for crashing the meeting. When we're done," he added with a sly grin, "you'll never have to worry about your Master again."

"You'll wait until he's away from the compound?" That was the first time since the meeting had started that Riley heard fear in Tessa's voice.

Phipps gave her an incredulous look. "Do you have to ask? No way are we giving him the home-field advantage. We want him out of his comfort zone."

Tessa passed him the slip of paper upon which she'd written the account number. "The second number is the account I'd like you to transfer my half into. You have two hours to accomplish that part of the deal. If I don't see the transfer, I'll tell the Master everything. And then your enemies won't have to worry about you ever again."

"And you think the man would believe you?" Phipps laughed. "I don't think so. Don't try threatening me, honey."

Riley pulled out his own cell phone and hit the necessary buttons to play back the conversation. He'd recorded every word. Phipps's face paled.

"Make the transfers within two hours," Tessa reiterated. "When they're done, I'll send you the details of the meeting and the scheduled transfers. That will be the end of our business dealings."

He smirked. "If you don't watch your back, it'll be the end of you."

Phipps walked away, giving his back as if he had no fear of Riley taking a shot at him. As if there was no chance any of the Master's soldiers were close by.

Riley's instincts were ranting at him again.

This was wrong.

Chapter Thirteen

Tessa's hands shook as she reached into the glove box for the cell phone the Master had given her. Their mission was complete with more than twenty-four hours to go. Would he trust Riley now? Remove the explosive device? Would Riley be able to help her and the children escape?

Tessa couldn't activate the evacuation plan…not with that thing around Riley's neck.

There was nothing else to do…except call him. Attempt to report in that Phipps had taken the bait. What did this prove? The Master knew Renwick was his enemy.

This was utterly insane. What had been the point? Was the Master planning an ambush for Renwick and his people? Had he been spurred to play out this possibly lethal ruse based on what she had told Riley to say to him? Would she be responsible for dozens of deaths?

Agony swelled inside her. They were all bad men. Monsters. She shouldn't feel any regret. Yet, she felt regret and confusion.

These people had been her family...no, they had stolen her from her family.

Tessa closed her eyes and forced the confusing thoughts away.

This wasn't her fault. The Master could have been planning a coup like this for some time and the opportunity had only now arisen. She was merely a pawn.

Like always.

"Used," she muttered. Used for bad things.

"You okay?"

She'd told Riley to head back to the compound. But she didn't want to arrive without calling first. The Master would know she was coming because of the tracking devices burrowed in her skin. But he didn't like to be surprised. He liked being prepared.

Tessa had the oddest feeling that he

expected she and Riley to fail or at least
to be down to the last minute accomplish-
ing the task he'd required they complete.
Had he hoped they would be terminated in
their attempts to carry out this operation?

Or maybe he'd hoped his enemy wasn't
quite so determined to get him. Had he
expected Riley's assertion to be proven
wrong?

Tessa didn't believe that. The Master had
made far too many enemies. Enemies who
had attempted to bring him down before.

That was the thing about being at the
top of the heap. Someone always wanted
to take your place.

She couldn't begin to analyze the Master.
He was unpredictable…and totally, crimi-
nally insane.

That realization settled heavily upon her.
A sane person didn't hurt people the way
he did. She swallowed back the misery
that hardened in her throat. She had to stop
him.

Another ring echoed in her ears, drawing
her back to the here and now. Why wasn't
anyone answering?

"Brooks."

It was about time. Tessa sat up straighter. "Brooks, this is Tessa. I need to speak to him."

"He's unavailable at the moment."

What? Another thread of confusion wound around her thoughts. "He's expecting my call. I have an update on the operation." Brooks had been there yesterday morning. He understood the magnitude of what she was doing.

"Does this mean that you and Smith have accomplished your mission?"

"Of course." That was a stupid question. Why would she call otherwise? "I'd like to speak to him, please."

"He asked me to relay the message that he will be expecting you tomorrow morning at eight."

"But—" She glanced at the steel band clamped around Riley's neck. "What about—?"

"That leaves sufficient time to take care of Mr. Smith's situation if that's your concern."

"No." Tessa's head shook of its own volition. "I need to speak with him, Brooks. We need to come back today. Now." She needed this man out of her way! Was this a power play on his part or had the Master actually told him to make her wait?

"That's out of the question," Brooks warned, his tone threatening. "Do not come here before eight tomorrow morning. Find some place to lie low until then. That's a direct order, Tessa. This would not be the time to start down the path of disobedience."

Before she could argue he severed the connection.

Tessa couldn't believe what Brooks had said to her. Why would the Master refuse to take her call? Something wasn't right.

A lot of things weren't right, she realized. The tiny fragments that didn't fit had been piling up...she should have stopped denying it and recognized the warning signs already.

"What happened?" Riley glanced from the road to her and back.

"He won't permit us to return before eight tomorrow morning." But she hadn't actually spoken to the Master. "Do you think Brooks and Howard or some of the others have staged some sort of takeover?" If the

Master had left the compound on business maybe…no, that didn't make sense. His deputies accompanied him when he was away.

"I think," Riley offered, "that we need to find out."

"But we can't go there," she cautioned. She had never disobeyed a direct order. Too often she'd seen the consequences suffered by those who dared. "He'll know we're coming." Damned tracking devices!

Riley pulled over to the side of the road. "I'll check in with Stark. Try to get some sort of status on the compound."

Tessa sat in a state of shock as Riley used his cell phone to contact his colleague. Those images of Sophie she'd held at bay for the past twenty-four hours came flooding in now. What if the Master took Sophie away? What if Tessa could never find her? The Master may have decided to punish Tessa. Killing her wouldn't be nearly so painful as taking Sophie…he would know that.

Devastation encircled her heart and tightened, tighter and tighter until it seemed to stop beating. She couldn't breathe…

couldn't think of anything but Sophie... her little girl.

Her little girl.

Not his.

Hers.

Riley closed his cell phone. She'd hardly been aware of his conversation.

"Stark says things are quiet at the compound. There have been no departures and no arrivals. None last night or this morning. The Master hasn't left the property since we made our exit twenty-two hours ago."

Some sense of relief lightened the pressure on Tessa's heart, allowing an erratic and desperate rhythm. "Why would he refuse to allow us to return?"

Glass shattered. Sprayed over Tessa's head.

"Get down!" Riley shouted.

The truck lunged forward.

Tessa cowered in the floorboard, her hands covering her head.

The truck swerved dangerously and rocketed forward faster and faster.

She prayed the old truck could take the abuse.

The rearview mirror burst, the wind-shield cracked.

Riley wrestled with the steering wheel as he weaved wildly to prevent being an easy target.

She had to help. "Give me the gun."

Riley ignored her.

"Give me the gun!"

The passenger-side mirror flew to pieces.

Riley dared to take a hand off the wheel and pass her the weapon. Their gazes locked for one second.

This was bad.

Tessa held the gun in both hands. She cleared her mind of thoughts of Sophie and pushed upward until her knees rested on the seat.

She fired at the SUV charging up behind them. The windshield of the SUV shattered. Riley swerved to the left. Tessa tumbled on top of him. A bullet whizzed past her shoulder. The air burst from her lungs. Too close.

She regained her balance, took another shot at the SUV roaring up behind them.

This time she aimed for a tire.

The SUV swerved.

She fired two shots into the front grill area. Then another at the windshield.

The SUV grew smaller and smaller as Riley pushed the truck forward.

Tessa took a breath.

"Hang on," Riley warned.

She clutched at the seat as he made a hard right. Then another abrupt left. Her body pressed against his shoulder.

Tessa crumpled into the seat. Her entire body shook.

"Where'd you learn to shoot like that?"

"The soldiers practice twice a week." She licked her lips and drew in a big, shaky breath. "The Master thought I needed to be skilled with a handgun."

"I'm impressed."

She shook her head. "I was lucky. The SUV was big and it was close."

"Some of the Master's people?" Riley asked.

Tessa pictured the SUV, straining to call to mind the details. "I can't be sure, but I don't think so. It was the same make and model but the window tinting was different." The Master had limousine-type tint put on all his vehicles. This SUV's wasn't as dark. But then she'd been operating on autopilot—otherwise she would have been terrified out of her mind.

"Renwick's people, maybe," Riley suggested.

"Maybe." She turned to the man behind the wheel. "Where'd you learn to drive like that?" He'd saved their lives.

"I wasn't always a good boy as a teenager." He shot her a smile. "Kansas City's finest still remember my name and the souped-up cars I drove."

Tessa relaxed marginally, allowed the phone call, the car chase, all of it to sink into her brain a little more deeply. Something was about to happen. She could feel it. The Master had a plan that didn't include her for some reason.

Had he discovered that she'd been planning an escape? There had been no evidence. She'd written nothing down. She'd said nothing to no one.

The key.

Except the hidden key. Had he discovered the key and realized it was part of a scheme?

Tessa turned to Riley. "We need to make a stop at a pharmacy."

He surveyed her head to toe between glances back at the road. "Are you hurt?"

The worry in his voice lightened the heaviness she felt just a tiny bit. "No, but there are things I need."

Perplexed, he asked, "Anything I need to know about?"

"Not yet."

She wasn't waiting for the Master to act. And she sure wasn't waiting until tomorrow.

Tessa had her own plan.

All she had to do was get Riley to go along with it.

9:02 a.m.—24 hours,
58 minutes remaining

TESSA HELD TIGHTLY TO THE bag of items she'd purchased at the drugstore. Riley had waited in the truck as she demanded. And, in part, due to the fact that he needed to watch for the cops. He didn't want to have to explain how their vehicle had accumulated so many bullet holes, much less why he was driving without a windshield or rearview mirror.

She'd asked him to return to the same motel they'd stayed in the night before. Prompts for an explanation had fallen on deaf ears.

Whatever she was planning, she had no intention of telling him just yet.

Once they were in the room with the door closed, she asked, "What did Stark say about the ambush?"

Riley tossed the keys and the now empty handgun onto the table. "That you were right. Nothing has moved at the compound."

Tessa extended the bag to Riley. "There's something I need you to do."

With mounting misgivings, he accepted the bag. "What's that?"

"Take them out."

He searched those pleading blue eyes. "That's not a good idea."

"It's the only way," she insisted.

"If we damage one and it stops working," Riley reminded her, "he's going to know what we're up to."

She grabbed the hem of her blouse and

pulled it over her head and off. "Then you need to be careful."

His fingers clenched on the bag. "This is crazy."

She shook her head. "Desperate, not crazy."

"We can wait him out," Riley argued. He didn't want to hurt her like this. And *this* was going to hurt like hell.

"Take them out," she demanded. "I need to get back onto the compound. Today, not tomorrow. Something's going down. I can feel it."

He couldn't argue her reasoning. The so-called master was up to something. "What's to keep Brooks or the others from finishing the job Renwick's people started?" Assuming it was Renwick's people who'd attacked them.

"We'll wait until they leave for the meeting. Whoever's left to guard the compound, I can handle. They'll be afraid to cross me."

"You're assuming the Master will go through with this mock meeting."

She nodded. "There has to be a reason he wanted Renwick to believe there was a meeting. My guess is he's setting the guy up to take him out."

Logical, Riley couldn't deny. Again, logic hadn't played a large role in any of this. "I don't think you fully comprehend what you're asking me to do."

"You're wasting time," she snapped. "Do it!"

He moved to the end of the bed where she sat. "This is crazy."

She said nothing.

Inside the bag he found hand sanitizer, gauze, tape, a medium-size protective pad, tweezers and a straight razor. And hairpins.

He shook his head, but opted not to waste any more time arguing with her. First, he cleansed his hands with the sanitizer, then he spread the pad on the bed and laid out the rest of the items atop it.

"Where do you want me to start?" Ross's tech had located one in her right shoulder, one in her right thigh, and another on her hip. How the hell was he supposed to do this?

"Start with the shoulder." She turned to the side. "I'm ready."

Riley tamped down the urge to stare at her breasts. Not an easy feat. "You'll need to pin up your hair."

"Yeah." She held out her hand for the pins.

He placed the hairpins in her palm and waited, while she tucked her hair into a haphazard twist. "Okay. Let's get this over with."

Riley scrubbed a hand over his jaw. They needed a doctor. A nurse at the very least.

"Hurry up," she ordered.

He sanitized his hands again and reached for the cutting tool. "Here goes." He used his fingertips to find the first device. The tech had pointed out the general location. There it was. Felt like a tiny kernel beneath the skin.

Riley picked up some gauze and held it against the skin near the intended incision site. He had to be out of his mind. He'd done this sort of thing for fellow soldiers in the military, but this was different.

This was Tessa.

He set the sharp edge against her skin and made the first incision. She tensed, but didn't make a sound. Using his fingers, he worked the tiny object until he ushered it to the surface. "Hold out your hand."

Her palm stretched open. He placed the first device there.

Moving quickly, he staunched the flow of blood as best he could with the gauze and taped it tightly into place. That would work for the moment.

"Stand up."

She pushed to her feet and was unfastening her jeans as he dropped to his knees next to her. Using her free hand, she slid the fabric down her right hip just far enough for him to do the job.

Her skin felt soft and warm...smooth.

Focus, man.

Taking the same steps, he eased the device from beneath the skin and placed it in her open hand with the first.

When he'd gauzed and taped the wound, she stared down at herself. "I think we made a strategic error. I should have taken off my jeans, too."

True. He blinked away the images her words evoked. "Put the tracking devices on the table and...pull off your jeans."

While she took care of that he washed his hands. The idea that it was Tessa's blood slipping down the drain with the soap and water made him feel queasy. She didn't deserve yet another indignity.

"Ready."

He turned around slowly, braced for seeing her in nothing but her underthings.

Didn't help.

As slender as she was, the subtle curves were more feminine than anything he'd ever seen. Her pale skin was smooth and flawless...a frown tugged at his brow. Except for a scar at the bikini line...just above the top of her low-rise panties.

As he walked closer to her he recognized that the scar was a surgical scar... his aunt had one in exactly that location. From when she'd had her last child...by caesarean section.

He kicked the questions he wanted to ask aside for the time being and knelt down on one knee to do what had to be done. This one took a little more manipulation, but he got it. Tessa didn't groan or whimper even once.

She was one brave woman.

When he'd properly dressed and taped each wound, he helped her pull on her clothes. She winced a couple of times during the process but never complained.

While Riley cleaned up the mess, she washed her hands and pulled the pins from her hair.

"You sure you're okay?"

She nodded. "Let's go."

He tossed the drugstore bag into the trash can and dusted his palms together. "We need to plan carefully. Rushing in would be a mistake."

"I have a plan." She stared at him defiantly. "We move in close and when Stark tells you that the Master has left the compound, we'll go in."

Sounded easy enough, but they needed ammo for the handgun. They needed to avoid being stopped for the condition of their vehicle.

There were numerous considerations that needed to be addressed.

"She's there," Tessa said, her voice small, her eyes wide with worry.

"You have a child?" The anguish in her eyes, on her face, tore at his heart. There were other reasons to have a scar in that particular spot, but having a child via caesarean section was by far the most likely.

"Her name is Sophie. She's almost three years old." Tessa blinked rapidly. "I've lost everything I ever had. I can't lose her."

Riley drew her into his arms and held her close. "I won't let that happen. I promise you. I won't let that happen."

His cell rang. He hated to let her go, but it would be Stark or Ross.

Riley kissed her forehead and stepped away to take the call. "Porter."

"Something's happening at the compound," Stark said. "Two SUVs have departed the garage. We couldn't determine how many passengers, but we believe there were more than two in each vehicle."

"We're on our way."

Riley grabbed his coat and the useless handgun. There was no time to make an ammo stop.

No time to prepare.

"What's happened?" Tessa demanded, looking up from tying her boots.

Riley passed along the news. Her eyes widened with fear.

"We have to get in there," Tessa said, abandoning her boot laces and grabbing her coat. "You know what they'll do if this is an evacuation."

Riley snatched up the keys and headed for the door. "Stark and Ross are prepared to move in. It's going to be okay."

She held his gaze a moment. "I hope that's a guarantee you can keep."

Chapter Fourteen

*10:27 a.m.—23 hours,
33 minutes remaining*

"Can't you go faster?" Tessa couldn't take the tension. She needed to be there *now!*

Riley glanced at her. "We're almost there. I'm pushing this old truck for all its worth."

He was. She knew this. But fear had disabled her ability to think rationally.

Had the Master left the compound? Had he taken Sophie? *Oh, please, please,* Tessa prayed, *don't let him have hurt the children. Please keep my baby safe.*

"Stark is meeting us at the stakeout perimeter," Riley explained. "There he is." He pointed to the road ahead where his colleague waited near an SUV.

Tessa felt a fraction of relief. "Tell him we have to get inside now."

Riley braked to a stop. Tessa bounded out of the truck. "We need to go in," she said, not waiting for Riley to make his way around the hood of the truck.

Stark held up his hands. "Let's talk about the status first. We don't know—"

"I have to get in there," Tessa interrupted. "I can't wait for your assessment or for anything else." Why weren't they listening to her?

"Tessa, listen to him," Riley urged. "Moving too hastily would be a mistake."

She opened her mouth to protest, but Stark reached for his phone. The words she'd intended to say died in her throat at the changing emotions on his face as he listened to the caller.

"Stop that vehicle," Stark said. "Stop it now."

Fear blasted through Tessa. "What vehicle?" Didn't he understand that if he tipped off the Master, the children would suffer the consequences? "You can't—"

"A third SUV," Stark said, cutting her off, "has exited the compound. Going west." He pointed in the direction on the other side of the compound and well beyond their position. "One of Ross's men spotted a man loading a child into the SUV after it exited the garage."

"Oh, my God." Tessa turned to Riley. "We have to get to that SUV. Sophie may be with them." She whirled back around to Stark. "Tell your men not to go near the SUV. I need to be the one."

"She's right," Riley said to Stark.

"Then go." Stark opened his phone to put through the needed call.

Riley had the truck moving before Tessa had fully closed her door. She braced a hand against the dash in preparation for a hard stop.

Just past the compound, maybe a mile, the SUV sat in the middle of the road. Two other SUVs had blocked its path, couldn't go forward, couldn't back up.

Riley hit the brake and shoved the gearshift into Park. Tessa wrenched her door open and jumped out.

"Tessa, wait!"

She ignored him. She had to get to that SUV.

Men wearing SWAT-type uniforms and gear spilled out of the SUVs blocking the road. Tessa ignored them as well. One grabbed her by the arm. The move tugged at the wound on her shoulder; she grimaced.

"Stay back, ma'am."

She tried to shake loose, didn't care about the pain in her shoulder or the gun in his hand. "Let me go!"

Orders to get out of the vehicle were shouted at the SUV.

Dear God, they were going to get the children killed.

Riley moved between her and the agent.

Tessa stared up at him, unable to breathe much less speak. As soon as he'd put his arm around her the other man released his grip on her arm.

"They know how to do this," Riley promised softly. "Let's stay calm and let them do their job."

Finally the front doors of the SUV opened.

Cries wafted through the air.

The children.

Tessa tried to pull away from Riley but he held on to her. Her heart twisted in agony.

Two men, both soldiers for the Master, hands held high, climbed out of the front seat.

The federal agents patted them down for weapons—both were carrying—and then forced them facedown on the pavement.

Two other agents opened the rear passenger doors.

Tessa started forward again; this time Riley allowed her to go. She rushed over to the SUV with him right behind her.

As the agents pulled the crying children from the back seat, Tessa counted. One... two...three...

"Clear," one of the agents shouted.

Tessa turned to Riley. "What does he mean?"

"He means the vehicle's clear, no other occupants."

But where was Sophie?

Tessa ran up to the man holding the oldest of the children. "Phoebe, where is Sophie?"

The little girl rubbed at her eyes with

both fists. "I don't know." Her face puckered; she reached for Tessa.

Tessa took the child into her arms. "It's okay. You'll be okay now." She swiped the tears from Phoebe's face. "You're sure you didn't see Sophie?"

Phoebe shook her head. "I think she's with the mommies."

Tessa's gaze flew to the woods surrounding the compound. That meant her daughter was still inside.

Tessa thrust the child at Riley.

She rushed up to the two soldiers who had been allowed to get back on their feet. Tessa got in the face of the first one she reached. "Where is the fourth child?" The voice didn't sound like hers. It sounded deadly, desperate. She didn't care.

The soldier shrugged and stole a look at the agents surrounding him. "I don't know what you're talking about, lady."

Tessa turned to the nearest agent. "Shoot him."

The agent looked at her as if she'd told him to shoot himself.

"Whoa," the soldier said. Then he caught

himself, adopted a cocky expression. "He can't do that."

"But I can."

Riley moved up next to Tessa, the empty gun in his hand, it's muzzle boring into the soldier's forehead.

Where was Sophie?

Tessa looked around. The children had apparently been loaded into another vehicle. They weren't in sight.

"Where's the other child?" Riley repeated.

Tessa stole a glance at the nearest agent. He made no move to stop Riley. Ross must have ordered them to stand down. They all wore wireless communication devices, which allowed for discreet communications.

"She must have hidden from us," the soldier said. "We tried to find all four of the kids after the others left, but we only found three."

"What were your orders?" Riley demanded.

The soldier shrugged. "To guard the compound until the Master returned."

Tessa shook her head. "You wouldn't dare take the children out of the compound unless ordered to do so." She couldn't call any of the soldiers by name—no one could except the Master and his deputies—but she knew their faces.

"He's not coming back."

The words truck terror in Tessa's heart. "Who's not coming back?"

"The Master."

First, he would never divulge his plans to a mere soldier. Second… "Why would you think that?" Her heart beat so hard she was sure it wouldn't survive the damage. Everyone around her surely heard it.

"They destroyed everything in his office."

The computers…files…the Master's entire professional history was in his private office. No one, not even Tessa, had ever been in his hidden office.

"How would you know?" she demanded. "You don't have access to his office."

"They left it open. Looks like a small bomb went off in there. Bits and pieces are everywhere."

Tessa's knees threaten to buckle. "What orders were you really given?"

The soldier glanced at the agent. "Evac orders."

Tessa swayed. Riley steadied her.

"What about the women?" Riley demanded, before Tessa could summon the words.

The soldier shrugged. "We left 'em. I wasn't about to kill a pregnant woman."

"But you took the children," Riley roared.

"They're just kids," the guy said, his attention split between Riley and the agent.

Fury exploded in Tessa's bones, resurrecting her courage. "Liar," she accused. "You took the children so you could sell them."

Riley dropped the impotent weapon to his side. "Get these scumbags out of my sight."

Tessa tugged at his jacket. "We have to find Sophie." The patients had likely tried to hide. Since Sophie was the youngest, they may have taken her into hiding as well. Tessa prayed that was the explanation.

"Come on," Stark said, drawing their attention to him. "We'll take this SUV."

Tessa's entire body shook as she climbed

into the backseat of one of the SUVs belonging to the federal agents. Riley kept looking back at her from the front seat as Stark drove to the compound's security gate.

The gate stood open.

More of that crushing fear pressed down on Tessa.

"Security has been disabled." The words came from her, but sounded like those of a lost child.

She sent another prayer heavenward. *Please let Sophie be safe.*

An explosion vibrated the air. The SUV shook.

"What the hell was that?" Stark demanded, hitting the brakes.

They were halfway up the drive to the house. No screams. No women running from the house. From what Tessa could see through the trees, the house was still standing. What in the world had just happened?

Riley and Stark were climbing out of the vehicle. Stark was speaking to someone on his cell phone.

"Did the evac have a destruction mode?"

Tessa got out more slowly, her mind still focused on the house.

"Tessa." Riley shook her. "Does the house have a destruct mode included in the evac plan?"

She looked into his eyes, saw the fear.

"I don't know." She knew there were steps to prevent anyone from finding incriminating information.

"We need a bomb squad," Stark was telling someone.

Tessa started running.

She didn't remember deciding to do so. Riley was yelling something at her back, but she just kept going. She had to find Sophie...and the women.

He caught up to her at the front steps of the house.

"You can't go in there until we assess the danger."

"Sophie and the others are in there!" Was he out of his mind?

"Stark and I are going in."

As he said the words Stark rushed up the steps and through the open door.

"Stay here," Riley ordered.

Tessa watched him disappear into the house.

Riley wouldn't know where to look.

More agents were rushing around the property, two more went inside.

The smell of devastation lingered in the air. The explosion had destroyed the massive garage that sat to the left of the main house.

Another boom rent the air. The ground shook beneath Tessa's feet.

The house shuddered.

She rushed inside. "Sophie!"

Riley appeared at the library door. "Basement's clear!" His gaze landed on her. "Get out of the house, Tessa!"

Another agent shouted that the kitchen was destroyed.

Tessa hit the stairs running. Riley was right behind her. "Tessa!"

"Clear," Stark announced, meeting them on the landing of the second floor.

"Their room is on the third floor," Tessa said, rounding the newel post and heading that way.

A strong grip pulled her back. "We go first," Riley warned.

She let them, but she remained right on their heels.

"Megyn!" Tessa had not been permitted to use the women's names. She hadn't even known their names until they began to trust her enough to tell her. Using their names when no one was around seemed to have comforted them. The Master insisted they be referred to as the patients. "Shelley!"

Riley and Stark echoed the names, moving from room to room.

Where were the women? "Lorie! Amanda!"

Desperation made Tessa's chest hurt.

There was nothing left except the fourth floor, the Master's living quarters. His office had been destroyed, but his bedroom suite hadn't been mentioned.

Tessa headed that way.

"Damn it, Tessa," Riley growled as he passed her, taking the steps two at a time.

The landing opened up to a large space. Tessa checked the closet. Riley and Stark surveyed the damaged office and the rest of the area.

"They aren't here." A horrible epiphany dawned. "Where was the other explosion?"

"The kitchen," Riley said. "Part of it is now in the basement."

If the women were in the kitchen…

Sophie.

"Hold up." Stark pressed his fingers to the earpiece he wore. Several seconds passed and he said, "Roger." His gaze connected with Tessa's. "They found the women. They were trying to escape through the woods."

Tessa didn't ask about Sophie. She had to be with the women. Tessa refused to believe anything else. She flew down the stairs, not slowing for anything. She hit the front door at a run.

Two agents were ushering the women down the long drive, away from the house.

"Megyn!" Tessa didn't stop running until she'd reached them. "Where's Sophie?" Her lungs couldn't take in enough air.

Megyn stared at Tessa for a long moment, her lips trembling, her face white as a sheet. "He took her, Tessa. The Master took Sophie with him. They're gone."

The world seemed to narrow in on Tessa… narrower and narrower…until there was nothing but Megyn's words echoing in her ears.

Sophie was gone.

The Master had taken her.

Chapter Fifteen

12:05 p.m.—22 hours,
30 minutes remaining

Riley wished there was something he could say but there was nothing.

Tessa sat in the SUV, staring at the cell phone the Master had given her. She had tried calling him and his deputies at every number she knew but had gotten no answer. Agent Ross had placed a tracing device on her phone in case she was contacted.

The women and children had been transported to a New Orleans hospital where they were being examined and treated if necessary. Agent Ross's special agent-in-charge had arrived to ensure the families were notified and interviews were properly conducted.

All the victims held at the compound were accounted for except little Sophie.

Riley climbed into the driver's seat next to Tessa and sat for a moment before speaking. "I know we've been over all this before, but I want you to think long and hard about places you've been with him. Other transfer locations. Secondary residences. Vacation spots. Has he visited other associates? Any family?"

"We were his family."

The hollow sound of her voice widened the crack in his already damaged heart. "He has a name. He was born somewhere. Most likely he has relatives somewhere."

"The only name I know is Master. He never spoke of family or places." She leaned her head against the seat. "We rarely went to transfer locations. The one in Chicago was an exception because of the murder."

Riley studied her weary profile. "Murder?"

She nodded. "The man in charge of operations there, Lane, I believe, purchased a child from a man who had tried to kill his wife. He ended up dead for his trouble."

"The Master didn't make it a habit of

buying children from murderers?" Give the man a gold star. Riley was aware of the murder...that tragic event had ignited the case that had brought him here.

"Too much risk. He prefers clean takes, typically from low income or at-risk families. The kind who don't get as much support from the police."

"What about you?" Tessa's family was upper-middle class, pillars of the community.

Tessa stared out at the winter sun for a time, then said, "He said he knew I was his from the moment he saw me. He could think of nothing else. I was to be his eternal companion."

Riley stretched his neck. With all that was going on he'd had no time to consider that the damned device locked around his throat was ticking down to a deadline. *Dead* being the operative word. The question he wanted to ask Tessa was actually none of his business, but he needed to know...for reasons that were beyond reasonable.

She turned to him, studied his face a moment before settling her gaze on his. "Not his mate in the physical sense," she said. "His soul mate. Emotional mate. A life companion."

More that didn't add up. "What about Sophie?"

Tessa looked away. "She's his daughter, but she was conceived in the same manner as the others."

"So you didn't have a physical relationship."

"Not even once."

Riley parked his hands on the steering wheel just to have something to do with them. According to the file he'd read, Tessa's family and friends had all stated the same when it came to her personal conduct. Good girl. Never got into trouble. Rarely dated. Had scarcely been kissed. Was it possible that she had never had sex?

Why the hell was he worried about that right now?

A realization slammed into his gut. "Is there or was there ever anyone else like you? A soul mate for the Master, I mean?"

She shook her head. "Brooks and Howard didn't like it. They said I came between them and the Master. But they got over it eventually."

"Then…" the wheels stared to turn in Riley's head "…that means he's not likely to take losing you so well. Maybe that's why he took Sophie. For leverage to get you back."

Their gazes met. She recognized the merit in his theory.

A chime pierced the air. Tessa sat up straighter, stared at the caller ID. "It's him," she breathed the words.

Riley jumped out of the SUV and waved to Ross and Stark to alert them to the call. He turned back to Tessa. "Answer it."

"Hello." Her voice shook a little.

Ross rushed over with an earpiece that would allow Riley to listen in on the conversation.

"Where is Sophie?" Tessa demanded.

"She is safe with me, of course," he assured her with sugary kindness. "It was necessary to move her away from the danger."

"I don't understand what's happening," Tessa said. "Brooks refused to allow me to speak to you. When I returned to the compound police were all over the place. I don't know what to do."

"I've lost your signal, Tessa," he said, the warmth of his tone going ice-cold. "How did that occur?"

"It's the FBI agents," she said, lowering her voice to a whisper. "They forced me to allow their removal. They said it was for my own safety. They're watching my every move. How do I get away?"

Good girl. Pride swelled in Riley's chest. They had gone over certain key phrases she needed to say if he called. So far she'd remembered every single one.

"Are you sure they're not listening?" he asked, a hint of skepticism detectable.

"I don't think so. I didn't tell them about this phone. Smith didn't, either." She sighed audibly. "Unless he has since they've been interrogating him."

"You and Smith did a good job with your task," he said. "All went exactly as planned with Renwick." Tessa's gaze collided with Riley's.

She moistened her lips. "Then why did you leave me? I followed your orders. It required two meetings but we accomplished our goal and then Brooks wouldn't let me speak to you."

"Two meetings?" the Master asked.

Riley had reminded Tessa to mention a second meeting in case anyone had been keeping an eye on them when they met with Stark and Ross at the old factory.

"The first was with some of Renwick's lower-level soldiers. It was a waste of time. I didn't like the idea. Smith is not as reliable as he claimed. That's why I have to hurry. If he tells them everything they'll never let me go."

Riley gave her the thumbs-up for that last line. Award-winning performance for sure.

"Tessa," the Master said, "I want you to think back to when you first became mine."

Riley wanted to puke.

"Yes."

"There was a place you loved to visit. Remember?"

Several beats of silence passed. "By the water? Yes, yes, I do remember."

"Yes, that's the one."

"Tell me what to do."

"Be there at midnight. Sophie and I will be waiting for you."

"Please, may I speak to her?"

The connection severed.

Tessa turned to Riley. He nodded.

She climbed out of the SUV and came around to where he stood. "Do you think we can trust him?"

"Not at all," Riley said, giving her the truth. "But we'll be ready for whatever he has planned."

"Ms. Woods."

She turned to Agent Ross. "Yes?"

"We need to have a strategy meeting and prepare for the next phase of the operation."

Stark joined them. "I just got a call from Simon." Simon Ruhl, the second in command at the Colby Agency. "He has been interfacing with your folks at the lab here in New Orleans," he said to Ross. "Between Jim Colby's findings and Simon's coordination skills, they believe they may have found a way to unlock the band." This he directed to Riley.

Relief inched its way up Riley's spine. "Sounds good to me."

"Why don't you and Stark go to the lab?" Ross suggested. "Ms. Woods and I will begin developing tonight's strategy at the temporary command center." A command center had been set up in a nearby church that had been closed for years.

Riley shook his head. "I'm not leaving, Tessa. They can come to us, or they'll just have to wait until this is over."

"Porter," Stark countered, "you're not being reasonable. That thing might not continue to be stable. We need to see what we can do now. The lab would be the safest environment for that."

"You should go," Tessa said. "The longer you're burdened with that thing the bigger the risk."

"If I go—" Riley stood his ground "—she goes."

"Fine," Ross relented. "We'll convene a strategy meeting at the lab."

Maybe Riley was being unreasonable, but he wasn't allowing Tessa out of his sight.

Just last week an agent from the Chicago Bureau had double-crossed Trinity Barrett. Most of the FBI agents across the nation were the best law enforcement officials to be found. But as with anything else, occasionally a bad apple could be found in the barrel.

Ross pulled out his cell. "Ross."

They all waited for him to finish the call. Even the air seemed to still as if the world knew that whatever the call was about it couldn't be good.

"Keep me informed," he said before ending the call. He looked from Stark to Riley, then Tessa. "There was an explosion across town. Six people are dead. One of them is a man named Phipps. The others haven't been identified."

Tessa's gaze shot to Riley's. The bastard had set up Renwick and his people. None of this had happened by chance.

Stark clapped Riley on the shoulder. "Come on. Let's get out of here." He headed for the SUV in which Riley and Tessa had been sitting. "You two can ride with me."

Riley, for one, would be grateful to be away from this place.

Jefferson Parish Crime Lab, 1:38 p.m.—20 hours, 22 minutes remaining

TESSA WATCHED FROM THE safety of the viewing room. Riley sat on a stool in the center of a sealed and reinforced room designed for defusing and deactivating bombs. A technician dressed in protective gear stood by in preparation for the attempt.

"A number of prints were lifted from the cell phone at our first meeting," Ross explained. He and Stark waited with Tessa in the viewing room. "None were in the system except yours. So we had no choice but to treat each of the other two individual prints as potentials."

"One set probably belongs to Howard," she noted, her mind not really on the discussion but on the man beyond the shatterproof glass. Funny, she didn't know Howard or Brooks by anything other than those names. She had no idea if those were surnames or first names. The soldiers were all simply "soldier" to her. The women, the patients, she had learned their names, but only in secret.

She had no idea who the Master was. Not his name or where he was from. She only knew him. The evil, heinous monster who had stolen nearly six years of her life. Had stolen far more from too many victims to count.

"We've made a sort of skin that mimics each one. The material has components of plastic, but it's incredibly pliable. This technology is still somewhat experimental, but it's our best shot at turning this thing off."

"If there's a safety feature built in?" She knew the answer but she wanted to hear Ross say as much.

"Investigator Porter is aware of the risk."

Tessa's heart lurched as the technician reached toward Riley's throat. He was the savior she had prayed for. The hero that had refused to let her down.

Now his life was at risk because of her.

A dangerous game masterminded by a ruthless monster.

"He's trying the first option now," Ross commented.

Tessa held her breath.

The seconds felt like hours.

Then the tech glanced toward the viewing glass and shook his head.

Tessa wasn't sure whether to be relieved or terrified.

"Now, he'll try the second one."

More of those trauma-filled seconds elapsed.

The tech shook his head once more.

It was over. There was nothing they could do.

Riley's only chance at surviving was finding the Master.

Tessa turned to Ross. "What if we can't find him?"

Ross didn't have to ask who she meant. "Then we'll try a more aggressive technique."

He didn't need to explain. She understood that by aggressive he meant dangerous.

The next forty-five minutes were a blur to Tessa. The agents prepared and reviewed a strategy. More agents were called in, but no local law enforcement in an effort to keep security tight.

Through all of it Tessa couldn't block the worries that despite the evacuation, the Master could still have someone watching her.

If he discovered she was lying to him she would never see Sophie again and Riley would die.

If he got even a whiff of a setup the meet would not happen.

"We need to add an escape to this strategy," Riley announced.

Tessa perked up. He'd read her mind! "I agree."

The agents around the room looked at Riley then at her as if they'd both gone over the edge.

"If this so-called Master decides Tessa has lied to him and that she's working with the enemy, he'll abandon the meet. We have to assume he may have someone watching her." Riley shook his head. "It wouldn't have been too difficult for anyone to have watched today's activities from an undetectable distance."

"Porter and Tessa are right," Stark chimed in. "We need to stay in character here. To Tessa—" he gestured to her "—we're the enemy. Anyone watching needs to observe that relationship in Tessa's actions."

The shaking started out of the blue. Maybe the events of the past twenty-four hours had caught up with her. Whatever it was, she couldn't keep her knees from bouncing. She clasped her hands together to control their shaking.

Riley stood. "We done here?"

"I suppose we are," Ross said reluctantly.

"I'll need a weapon and a charged cell phone." He glanced at Tessa. "Tessa will need a weapon as well. She's a crack shot."

Tessa pushed back her chair and stood on shaky legs. "I'll need a change of clothes." The Master was obsessed with cleanliness.

Her bag was God knew where.

She had to do every step of this right.

No matter the cost to her.

She had to save her daughter...and Riley.

STARK ROLLED THROUGH THE lab facility's security gate. "Any particular direction?"

"Head southeast toward Mandeville," Tessa suggested.

Riley nodded. "That'll put us in the right direction."

Tessa gazed out the window, not really seeing, just staring mindlessly. Sophie would be wondering where she was. She hated when Tessa was separated from her for any length of time.

"You okay?"

She shifted her attention to Riley and nodded. Talking wasn't something she felt prepared to do just now. What she wanted to do was cry. Like she did in the beginning when she'd first come to belong to the Master. She had cried so hard. At one point she'd thought the tears would never go away.

Finally, the endless river had dried up and she had accepted her fate.

Fate had not been kind to her.

Her gaze settled on Riley. Until now.

Courage solidified inside her. She was no kid anymore. The opportunity had arrived and she had to make it work.

No more feeling sorry for herself.

"This is good," Riley said to Stark. He glanced back at Tessa. "Brace yourself."

Stark hit the brakes, sending the SUV into a sideways skid. As soon as the vehicle squealed to a stop, Riley grabbed Stark by the jacket.

"This is going to hurt me more than it does you." Then he slammed his fist into the other man's jaw.

Suddenly the driver's-side door opened and Riley pushed Stark out as he scrambled into the driver's seat.

Riley jabbed the accelerator and spun away, tires squealing.

Tessa turned back to check on Stark. He got up, dusted off his clothes and immediately pulled out his cell phone.

"Are you sure he'll be okay?"

"Ross isn't far behind us. He'll stay out of sight until enough time has passed for him to have gotten a call and arrived on the scene, but he's close enough to keep an eye on Stark."

Tessa climbed over the console to settle in the front passenger seat. Fontainebleau State Park was half an hour from New Orleans proper. Somewhere along the route they would pick a motel and wait.

"You're sure about this location?" Riley asked, no matter that his colleagues had asked fifty times already.

"I'm as sure as I can be," she offered, a

tiny voice screaming at her that this was wrong. So wrong. She trusted Riley completely, but she alone could do what had to be done.

It was the only way to ensure her daughter's survival. And Riley's survival. "The old sugar mill in the park," she explained. "He took me there once. I was fascinated by the history." It was the only thing that had felt real to her at the time. The Master had mistaken her fascination for acceptance and affection.

Playing along had been her saving grace.

For five years and eight months hatred had festered inside her.

As soon as she knew that Sophie was safe and Riley was free of danger, Tessa had a single goal.

To kill the bastard.

6:45 p.m.—15 hours, 15 minutes remaining

RILEY CHECKED THE WEAPONS. He'd wanted Tessa to agree to wear a vest, but she had refused. The Master would notice. They'd stopped at a discount store and picked up a change of clothes and toiletries. Ross had provided a first-aid kit for redressing her wounds.

He glanced at the bathroom door. She was still in the shower.

This motel was a step up from the last one, but that wasn't saying a lot. Stark had checked in with Riley, as had Ross. Four agents and Stark had entered the park from different positions and taken up posts within a visual range of the sugar mill.

Riley had his doubts as to whether the man would show. He seemed damned high up the food chain to take a risk this dicey.

To that end, a secondary perimeter had been established in the event he only came close enough to watch. Any vehicle that came anywhere near Fontainebleau Park wouldn't be leaving without a search they wouldn't even know about. The vehicles would be scanned via a new, cutting-edge X-ray technology.

The Bureau had pulled out their best.

Whether it would be enough or not, Riley wasn't prepared to wager.

His top priority was to keep Tessa safe and to get the child back.

The feds would have to worry about this so-called Master. They had succeeded in dismantling his network to some degree already. The feds had a lot more information than before. It was a major step in the right direction.

The bathroom door opened. "It's all yours," Tessa announced, emerging amid a cloud of steam.

Riley grabbed his new clothes. "Thanks."

He worked hard at not staring at her body wrapped in nothing but a towel.

"I wanted to talk to you before this gets too crazy," she said.

He gestured to the chairs at the table near the window. "You want to sit?"

She shook her head. "This will only take a moment."

"Okay." He hoped she wasn't about to reveal something to him that he couldn't fix at this stage in the operation.

She reached up, touched the steel band around his neck. "I'm sorry about this."

"It's not your fault." He hated that she carried that burden. She was a victim just like the others.

"Maybe not, but I'm sorry all the same." She finger-combed her damp hair. "I regret that my daughter is in danger…that I didn't do something soon enough." She closed her eyes and shook her head. "I wish I had been stronger, smarter."

That was enough. He took her by the shoulders, careful of the wound on the right one, and gave her a little shake. "You didn't do this. *He* did. No matter what happens, you have to remember that."

She nodded. "Can you do one thing for me?"

"You want me to redress your wounds?"

"Not now. After you shower."

"All right." He knew a lot of things he would like to do but they were all out of line. "Name it. What can I do for you?"

"I need you to kiss me." She searched his eyes. "A real kiss. I need to feel something real."

He opened his mouth to argue, but she tiptoed and pressed her lips to his.

TESSA MELTED INTO THE KISS. His lips felt firm and warm. She smoothed her palms over his chest, clasped his strong arms. She wanted to explore all of him. His arms went around her and pulled her closer, pressing her body against his. The shock of sensations that went through her made her moan. She wanted more…so much more.

But the kiss would have to be enough.

He drew back, pressed his forehead to hers. "I think we should leave it right there…for now."

A smile tugged at her tingling lips. "Okay."

He kissed her forehead and headed for the shower. He paused at the bathroom door and winked at her. "We'll continue this later. For sure."

She nodded. "For sure."

When he'd closed the door, she quickly yanked on her clothes. Her shoulder stung when she pulled the sweater over her head, but she had no time to worry about that. As soon as her boots were on, she dragged on her coat and tucked the smaller of the two handguns into her coat pocket, then quietly slipped out the door.

Chapter Sixteen

Tessa unlocked the SUV and climbed into the driver's seat. She entered the address into the GPS, placed the keys on the console and hopped out.

Then she ran. As fast as she could in the direction of the convenience store two blocks away.

She would be picked up there.

Please let them be there already. She'd warned Brooks that she had at best six or seven minutes.

Her chest felt ready to explode by the time she hit the parking lot.

The SUV started rolling toward her at the same instant she recognized it.

Instinctively she went to the rear passenger door. Once she'd climbed in she came face-to-face with Howard and Brooks. Both glared at her from the front seat.

"Hurry," she urged Brooks, who looked exactly as if he was not happy to see her. Not happy at all. She imagined they had both thought they were rid of her for good.

The two men exchanged a look and Brooks did as she ordered.

Tessa closed her eyes and prayed they would take her to the location she'd expected. The one she hadn't told Riley or the others about.

This was the only way. There was absolutely no possibility that the Master would have come with feds spread out all over the place. He had too many contacts for her to take the risk that he wouldn't hear about what was going down.

She strained to see through the dark tint. So far they appeared to be going in the expected direction.

To the hiding place. To her knowledge, no one knew about the place except Brooks, Howard and her.

It was a secondary safe house of sorts. She had kept that place from Riley and from the others...she couldn't risk Sophie's safety...not for anything. The Master was too smart. He would have known they were coming. This was the only way.

The Master would lie low there until he felt it was safe to move. Then he would set up business someplace else. He was like a ghost. No one knew him, much less where he'd come from. How could any law enforcement agency, no matter how elite, find a ghost?

So Tessa had decided to go to him...as if nothing had changed. It was the only way.

The handgun felt heavy in her pocket.

He would never imagine that she would attempt to kill him. She'd played her part too well for too long.

But that was over.

Tessa was finished waiting for fate to do right by her. Tonight she was going to make her own destiny.

7:20 p.m.—14 hours,
40 minutes remaining

RILEY TUGGED ON HIS JEANS, then scrubbed his damp hair with the towel once more. He touched his lips, thought of that kiss. The idea that Tessa had been a victim for so long and was clinging to the first safety she'd felt in all those years had prompted him to temper the kiss. He wouldn't take advantage of her desperation.

Later, if she still wanted to pursue a relationship, he was definitely game.

But not until she had her life back. Not until she'd figured things out.

He dragged on his sweater and threaded his fingers through his hair. When he reached for the door, he hesitated. He hoped she wasn't regretting that kiss already. Feeling embarrassed or uncomfortable in any way was the last thing he wanted for her.

She'd suffered enough already.

"We could order—"

Riley stalled. He surveyed the entire room before he allowed his brain to make the only feasible assessment.

The room was empty.

Fear bolted through him. He sprinted to the table. The keys were gone.

"Damn it!" He jerked the door open and stepped outside.

To his surprise the SUV sat right in front of the door.

If she hadn't driven away…

She'd given her location, and they'd picked her up.

She'd taken the keys to keep him from following.

He grabbed his cell phone and entered Stark's number. Where the hell were his socks? Screw the socks. He grabbed his boots and tugged them on.

"Stark."

"She's gone."

"Where?"

"She must have given her location and they came for her while I was in the shower." He was a fool. A damned fool. He shouldn't have allowed her out of his sight.

"I'll meet you at—"

"Can't. She took the SUV keys."

"Hold on."

Riley pulled on this jacket while Stark spoke to someone else. Riley stormed out of the room and surveyed the darkness.

"Damn it," he muttered again.

"Porter," Stark said, "check the wheel

wells. Ross says they usually keep a spare key hidden on official vehicles."

"Give me a minute." Riley checked the front wheel well closest to the driver's-side door. Nothing. He moved to the rear. Bingo. "Got it."

"Do you have any idea where they would take her?"

Riley climbed into the seat. "Not a—" The keys lay on the console. She hadn't taken them. But why were they in the vehicle. "Hold up," he muttered to Stark. He looked around the interior. Nothing out of place. No note. Nothing. "She left the keys in the vehicle." He started the engine. Didn't make sense.

Stark provided a rendezvous location halfway between his position and Riley's. "On my way," Riley assured him.

He backed up and pulled out of the lot.

It wasn't that he didn't understand her motivation. Her daughter's life was at risk. She knew better than anyone how the bastard thought. Didn't take a genius to figure out she worried that he would recognize the setup and fail to show.

She'd done what she thought was necessary to save her child. Riley just wished she had included him.

"Turn left in two blocks."

The voice startled him. He stared at the GPS built into the dash. The map on the screen indicated that he should turn left.

Still confused, he missed the turn.

"Recalculating," the GPS voice announced.

He stopped in the middle of the street and pressed a couple of buttons. The final destination appeared on the screen.

A broad smile spread over Riley's lips.

"Brilliant, Tessa."

He hit the call button and got Stark back on the line. "I know where she's going."

All they had to do was get there…fast.

8:00 p.m.—14 hours remaining

TESSA BENT DOWN AND PLACED a soft kiss on her baby's silky blond head. The urge to gather her into her arms was overwhelming. But she didn't want to wake her. The events that would occur next were not fit for a child to see.

Tessa turned to exit the bedroom, and

the Master waited for her in the doorway. "Thank you for keeping her safe."

He stepped aside, allowing her out of the room. She closed the door behind her.

"She's our child. Of course I would protect her, just as I'll protect you."

She looked into his eyes, forced all the gratitude she could muster into hers. "You're my savior. I'd be lost without you."

He'd called himself that five years and eight months ago. The word tasted bitter on her tongue.

"Come." He took her arm and wrapped it around his. "We'll decide where to start our new family." He patted her arm. "The entire world is open to us."

He had ordered Brooks and Howard outside while he and Tessa spoke privately. The two were his only trusted followers. One or the other would be standing guard around the clock.

Not that anyone was likely to stumble upon this rustic cabin. It was so deep in the swamp. Reachable only by boat. She hated this place.

But Tessa was no fool. She'd gotten a

head start but she still provided a backup opportunity.

Riley wouldn't fail her.

"Have you eaten, Tessa?"

Food was the dead last thing on her mind. "I can't remember. Actually I'm very hungry. I hadn't even thought about it until now." She wasn't but since Brooks had taken her coat, she needed to get her hands on a weapon. The kitchen was the most likely place.

He escorted her to the kitchen, his hand firmly on her arm. She shuddered inside, wanted to scream just being near him. A little bit longer, she reminded herself. She had to stay calm.

"I prepared a lovely salad," he said as he removed the items from the fridge. "This time of year it's so difficult to find fresh greens."

She made an agreeable sound. When he picked up a broad-bladed knife and sliced a serving of bread, her attention locked on the knife. He placed it on the counter next to the sink behind him.

Moving around the table to stand beside him, she said, "That looks wonderful."

He lifted a forkful of salad to her lips. She forced her mouth open and accepted the generous bite.

"Quite wonderful, isn't it?"

She chewed and made another of those agreeable sounds. Almost choking, she managed to get the lump down.

He leaned against the sink counter and studied her as she forced herself to take another bite.

"I've given you everything, Tessa."

She nodded. Swallowed. The tension inside her rushed to the next level. The evil in his eyes told her that he was not fooled by her at all.

"I took you from a hideous life and offered you the world. Gave you Sophie." He shook his head. "And still you deceived me. Did you really believe that an old dilapidated truck would be your salvation?"

He had found the key! He'd known… This entire chain of events had been a test. The end of his time here. Now he was tying up loose ends.

"Phipps told me how that man—Smith— looked at you." The Master shook his head. "Before he died he swore that you looked at Smith in a similar manner. You know very well that I will not tolerate deception of any sort."

Tessa didn't bother to argue. Nothing she said or did would change the decision he had made.

He removed a small packet from the pocket of his trousers. "I don't want this to be messy or distasteful. I want to leave you as beautiful as you are this minute." He extended the packet to her. "This will end your life quietly. You may spend your final moments with Sophie, watching her sleep."

The clear plastic packet contained a dose of lethal poison. She'd seen him hand it out to his soldiers. She also knew exactly what it did and how fast it worked.

"It's a slow dissolving capsule," he assured her. "You'll have a few moments."

Tessa restrained the fear. "I'll need water."

"Of course." He turned to the sink.

Tessa dropped the packet, reached around him and grabbed the knife.

He dropped the glass. Whipped toward her. Grabbed her by the throat.

She plunged the knife into his stomach.

Shock claimed his expression. His fingers loosened.

She stumbled back. Bumped into the table.

He lunged toward her again. Her fingers locked around the knife and she twisted the handle, shoved it upward.

A sound gurgled from his throat. He collapsed against her.

She pushed him off.

Her gun. She needed the gun.

Take a breath. Check the room first. She peeked around the corner of the door leading from the kitchen to the living room.

Empty.

She grabbed her coat from the chair and fished out the gun.

Where was her cell phone?

Other pocket.

She fumbled for the phone. Tucked it into her jeans pocket.

Sophie.

She rushed to the first of the two bedrooms. Wrapped her sleeping child in the wool blanket atop her and took a breath.

Where were Howard and Brooks?

Not far away, she could count on that.

Tessa eased into the living room, the weapon in one hand, Sophie in the other arm. Moving soundlessly, she leaned against the front door and listened.

The two were chatting on the porch.

Howard said something about having to do some business. Man-talk for tramping through the woods to urinate on a tree.

Brooks told him to hurry up and get back.

The door knob twisted.

Tessa stepped back.

The door opened and Brooks started.

"Give me your weapon and you'll live through this," she warned.

Fury whipped across his face. "What have you done?"

"Do it now!" Tessa warned, not wanting to raise her voice.

Brooks reached for the gun in his waist-band.

Tessa fired, hitting him center chest.

His gun discharged into the floor.

Sophie jerked in Tessa's arms as the man crumpled, following the path of the bullet.

Fear pounded in Tessa's ears. She patted Sophie's back. Had to think.

No way did Howard not hear that.

She ran out the door.

Where was the SUV?

Wait. She had no keys.

Probably in Brooks's pocket. Did she take the time to dig for them...or run?

Run!

Tessa dashed down the steps and toward the crooked dirt road that had brought them here.

"What the hell?"

Howard.

She plunged into the darkness of the woods, praying she remembered her way well enough not to end up in the swamp.

The sound of Howard's gun discharging shattered the silence. Bullets hit trees all too close.

Tessa kept running.

Her boots crunched in the snow. This deep in the woods it was still up to her ankles.

Don't look back. Don't stop.

If she could lose him, she could call Riley.

If she didn't freeze to death first.

But he would be en route by now.

Sophie whimpered.

Tessa held her tighter and whispered softly to her as best she could without slowing her dead run.

Her boot caught on something. Tessa plunged forward. She twisted her body so as to land on her back.

Not even the snow softened the impact. The breath whooshed out of her.

"You bitch!"

Tessa pushed Sophie away from her.

Howard lunged on top of Tessa. She struggled to jam the gun into his torso. A fist impacted her jaw.

"You are dead," Howard roared.

She tried to knee him in the groin.

He dodged, jabbed the muzzle of his weapon into her belly. "Die b—"

His weight suddenly lifted. His weapon discharged. She saw the flash from the muzzle. He fell backward.

Tessa lay there in the snow unable to move.

Was she hit?

The muzzle hadn't been pointed at her when it fired.

"Tessa." Riley was suddenly kneeling next to her. "Are you all right?"

"I think so," she managed.

He pulled her to a sitting position.

Stark and another man were holding Howard on the ground. He was screaming about all the information he knew. Where other children were being held.

"Sophie." Tessa scrambled to her knees and gathered her baby girl into her arms. Sophie was sobbing quietly. Tessa uncovered her face and kissed her cheek. "It's okay now, baby."

She held her child close against her chest and smiled up at the man who had saved her.

It really was okay now.

The beam of a flashlight glinted against the metal around Riley's throat.

Dear God…the bomb.

Tessa pushed to her feet. "The Master's dead." She hadn't thought…what had she done?

"Where is he?" Riley asked, getting

to his feet and reassuring her with his hands.

How could he do that? His life was still in danger and he caressed her hair, touched her cheek. She had killed the man who held the key to Riley's life.

"He's inside…the kitchen." What had she done? What had she done?

"Let's get you in there," Stark said to Riley.

They trudged back to the cabin.

"Stay back, Tessa," Riley warned. "If this goes wrong, I don't want you within the impact radius. Or Sophie."

If it were just her…but it wasn't. She had to protect Sophie.

Tessa nodded.

Riley leaned down and kissed her cheek. "Don't worry," he murmured. "I'll be back for you."

Her lips trembled as the tears flowed down her cheeks.

"Let's move back, ma'am."

Tessa didn't know this agent, but he ushered her farther from the cabin.

Seconds turned to minutes…the minutes seemed to lapse into eternity.

Tessa did what she always did. She prayed.

She hugged her baby and hoped Sophie would have the opportunity to know Riley.

Tessa closed her eyes and imagined him hugging the little girl. Of her and Riley going together to be with her family.

"Tessa!"

Her eyes flew open.

Riley walked across the porch, toward her.

Was it over?

Her heart thudded hard.

She wanted to run toward him, but the agent held her back.

Riley walked straight up to her and smiled. "The Master's last act was to do the right thing. It's over. He can't hurt you or anyone else anymore."

Tessa ran into Riley's arms. She was free of that evil. Free to begin her life again. With her sweet daughter. And maybe with this wonderful man.

Chapter Seventeen

Chicago, Friday, January 1

Victoria Colby-Camp considered her reflection in the mirror. The red was nice. She'd tried on several dresses already, but she simply couldn't decide which one she wanted to wear.

She and her husband, Lucas, were going to a very special party tonight. Ian Michaels and his lovely wife, Nicole, were hosting a New Year's cocktail party for the entire agency.

Victoria smiled. The new year was off to a wonderful start. Waylon Smoltz, the man who had called himself the Master, was dead. His organization was being dismantled by the Bureau. The one key survivor, Howard Keats, one of Smoltz's deputies, was providing more evidence than anyone had dared to hope for. Hundreds of missing children were being tracked down. Emotion welled in Victoria's chest. She was so proud of the members of her agency for their part in that incredible feat.

Jim's team of former Equalizers were fully merged with the Colby Agency now. Things were running more smoothly than ever.

Her son had just yesterday sold the brownstone and the Equalizers name.

Lucas was spending several days per week at the agency. Both Victoria and Jim genuinely appreciated his incredible insights.

Victoria's two beautiful grandchildren were happy and healthy.

She couldn't ask for more.

The red silk dress, she decided as she went in search of shoes and a handbag.

Lucas was already waiting in the den.

But he was a patient man.

Red shoes, red handbag. She fished through the contents of her purse to transfer the essentials. A business card drifted to the floor. She picked it up to tuck it back into her purse. The card with the date and time of her doctor's appointment next week.

Victoria groaned. She deplored annual physical examinations. But it was necessary. Lucas would never let her miss one again.

With a last check of her hair, she was off.

"It's about time," Lucas said as she entered the den. He whistled. "You look fantastic."

She whirled around, letting the silky fabric swirl around her legs. "Thank you. So do you." Her husband looked exceptionally distinguished in his charcoal suit.

He helped her into her coat. "Did Jim tell you that Porter is spending the weekend with the Woods family?"

Victoria nodded. "He did. I think that's a wonderful idea. The transition will be difficult for Tessa. Riley will make a fine buffer." Victoria smiled. "That Sophie is a little doll."

"She is," Lucas agreed. He kissed his wife's cheek. "Let's go show these kids how we baby boomers party."

Victoria and Lucas might be getting older, but nothing was going to slow them down.

Together they were invincible.

Purvis, Mississippi

TESSA WATCHED FROM THE doorway as her parents played with Sophie. The little girl had only met them two days ago and already she loved them.

And they loved her.

An arm went around her neck and Tessa looked up at her brother. He smiled down at her. God, he'd gotten so tall.

"I missed you," he said quietly.

She nodded, tears stinging her eyes. "Not as much as I missed you."

He ruffled her hair with his fist like he used to do when she was a kid. "Karin's coming over after dinner."

Tessa smiled. She'd done a lot of that lately. "I can't wait to see her."

Her brother nodded. "She wanted to give us some time."

Tessa tiptoed and kissed his jaw. "I always knew you two would end up together."

"Yeah, right."

He wandered over to play with Sophie.

Tessa and her mother shared a smile.

Tessa wasn't sure her heart could take any more happiness. It was overwhelming... perfect.

Another warm body moved up beside her.

Riley.

He was a major part of that happiness. She watched him watch her family. "This wouldn't have happened without you." It was true.

He squeezed her hand. "I think you were on the right track. I just sped up the process."

"Maybe."

She studied his handsome face. The bruises from the beating he'd taken were pretty much faded now. She would never be able to repay him. She wanted him to stay... here. Forever. But he'd insisted they had to take this slow since she might feel otherwise when she got her bearings again.

Victims often grew attached to their rescuers, he'd explained. The way she felt might not last.

But it would.

Tessa knew it would.

She laced her fingers in his. "Just so you know," she said, "you're stuck with me."

He turned his face to hers, tried to hold back the smile toying with his lips but it wasn't working. "That's good because I have to tell you, I can't imagine my life without you."

She punched him in the arm with her free hand. "You could've told me that already."

He shook his head. "I had to give you time."

"Time." She shook her head. "I have a lot of lost time to make up for." Her tummy tingled at the idea of some of the things she would like to catch up on and experience for the first time with him.

"And you have my word that I'll be around for every minute of it…as long as you want me."

She tiptoed and whispered in his ear, "How about forever?"

He released her hand and draped his arm around her shoulders. "Deal…as long as we go real slow. You have college and lots of other stuff to do, too. I want you to have everything you missed."

"I'm holding you to it, mister." Tessa didn't care…as long as every step included Sophie and him. Her gaze settled on the people surrounding her daughter. And her family.

* * * * *

LARGER-PRINT BOOKS!

GET 2 FREE LARGER-PRINT NOVELS
PLUS 2 FREE GIFTS!

HARLEQUIN®
INTRIGUE®

Breathtaking Romantic Suspense

YES! Please send me 2 FREE LARGER-PRINT Harlequin Intrigue® novels and my 2 FREE gifts (gifts are worth about $10). After receiving them, if I don't wish to receive any more books, I can return the shipping statement marked "cancel." If I don't cancel, I will receive 6 brand-new novels every month and be billed just $4.99 per book in the U.S. or $5.74 per book in Canada. That's a saving of at least 13% off the cover price! It's quite a bargain! Shipping and handling is just 50¢ per book.* I understand that accepting the 2 free books and gifts places me under no obligation to buy anything. I can always return a shipment and cancel at any time. Even if I never buy another book from Harlequin, the two free books and gifts are mine to keep forever.

199/399 HDN E5MS

Name _____ (PLEASE PRINT) _____

Address _____ Apt. # _____

City _____ State/Prov. _____ Zip/Postal Code _____

Signature (if under 18, a parent or guardian must sign) _____

Mail to the **Harlequin Reader Service:**
IN U.S.A.: P.O. Box 1867, Buffalo, NY 14240-1867
IN CANADA: P.O. Box 609, Fort Erie, Ontario L2A 5X3

Not valid for current subscribers to Harlequin Intrigue Larger-Print books.

Are you a subscriber to Harlequin Intrigue books and want to receive the larger-print edition? Call 1-800-873-8635 today!

* Terms and prices subject to change without notice. Prices do not include applicable taxes. N.Y. residents add applicable sales tax. Canadian residents will be charged applicable provincial taxes and GST. Offer not valid in Quebec. This offer is limited to one order per household. All orders subject to approval. Credit or debit balances in a customer's account(s) may be offset by any other outstanding balance owed by or to the customer. Please allow 4 to 6 weeks for delivery. Offer available while quantities last.

Your Privacy: Harlequin Books is committed to protecting your privacy. Our Privacy Policy is available online at www.eHarlequin.com or upon request from the Reader Service. From time to time we make our lists of customers available to reputable third parties who may have a product or service of interest to you. If you would prefer we not share your name and address, please check here. ☐

Help us get it right—We strive for accurate, respectful and relevant communications. To clarify or modify your communication preferences, visit us at www.ReaderService.com/consumerchoice.

HILP10R

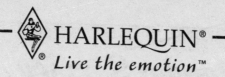